BLOOD TRAIL

Gardner Fox

BELMONT TOWER BOOKS • NEW YORK CITY

A BELMONT TOWER BOOK

Published by

Tower Publications, Inc.
Two Park Avenue
New York, N.Y. 10016

Copyright © 1979 by Tower Publications, Inc.

All rights reserved
Printed in the United States of America

chapter 1

The three empty cartridge shells reflected the firelight.

They stood upright on a flat rock a few feet from the small fire where a coffeepot rested at the edge of the burning branches. They were .44-.40 cases, polished and bright from long handling, and they had been fired so long ago the powder smell was gone from inside them.

The lean man hunkered down, a cup of coffee in his hand, not heeding the faint honking of the geese high among the clouds nor the chill wind whispering through the barren branches of the lodgepole pines which covered this high corner of the Ramparts. His gaze held only the three shells, and there was a brooding sadness in his eyes.

His hand went out to the first shell.

"Red Patsy," he whispered between his teeth, and his fingers closed down on the brass cylinder. He stared at it for a moment, then tucked it away in a pocket of his vest.

He was a tall man with sharp angles to his bronzed face and a wide mouth that showed inbred humor beneath its present bitter lines. He wore his black Stetson low over narrowed eyes with the same casual air with which he wore the faded black flannel shirt and dusty boots. A heavy shellbelt of expensive leather holstered a Frontier Colt revolver. The belt and the gun were the only clean, polished things about him.

He took the second shell off the rock.

For a moment he juggled it on a big palm before whispering, "Dutch Korman." Firelight built a redness along the cartridge as if some Blackfoot medicine man spell had imprisoned those darting tongues within the brass case. His eyes were turned inward, away from the reflected fire; he was seeing the big blond German standing in the New Mexico sunlight, his gunhand blurring. His ears heard the mocking laughter of long ago, and a wild savagery stirred along the channels of his blood...

They had been lying there in the tumbled rocks edging the prairie, their rifles thrust out in front of them, as he came cantering along the trail to Santa Fe. He was carrying more than forty thousand dollars in his saddlebags, money his guns had won for him over the past dozen years, money he was riding to turn over to the Territorial governor, as he had promised in his letter, so that he would come under the terms and conditions of the amnesty.

The governor was an Eastern man with a hunger to take his seat in the United States Senate. An amnesty for outlaws, a blanket pardon for those hardcases willing to turn in their guns and the loot of their outlaw years, was his way of insuring peace in his Territory. More than a dozen men, tired of the long riding and the lonely nights, had taken advantage of his offer. Abel Kinniston meant to be one of the wise ones. Until he rode into the ambush, that is.

He neither saw nor heard anything. Three bullets drove into his chest and hip and arm at the same time.

He went backward over the cantle, catching a glimpse of a big blond man with a sun-reddened face rising out of the rock clusters, laughing, and drawing his revolver amid a reeling maelstrom of blue sky falling in upon him.

They had come and stood over him, staring down upon him, and they had believed him dead, for though his eyes were open, something inside him had been paralyzed by their bullets so that he could not close his eyes nor blink them but lay looking up at the sky.

They had taken his saddlebags with the forty thousand dollars in them and they had ridden off across the flatlands. They believed Abel Kinniston to be dead; there was no need to waste another bullet on him.

He would have died, too, had not Old Tom found him and taken him to his hogan. Old Tom was an aged Navajo sheepherder who would not let even a dog die without trying to save its life. He had strapped Abel Kinniston on the back of his appaloosa and walked him to the dried chokecherry roots which, properly chewed to form a gummy paste, had stopped the flow of his blood. The Indian had dug out two of the bullets with his hunting knife while the lean man lay unconscious. The other bullet was somewhere back there on the cap rocks.

Two months later he found the three empty cases, there on the cap rocks where they had fallen. He had searched more than an hour before their telltale gleam in among the tumbled stones showed him where the men had lain in wait for him. He had picked up the shells and put them in his pocket.

The terms of the amnesty had run out by this time. Abel Kinniston was still a wanted man. Bitterness was a tiny flame inside him, making him live through those long hours when his life hung on a single heartbeat. Old

Tom did not believe he would live, and told him so when he was up and sitting in a chair.

Kinniston had grinned coldly, making the Navajo shiver. "I'll live," he promised, "leastwise, long enough to hunt them down."

"You know men shoot you?" Old Tom asked, sucking at his long-stemmed clay pipe.

"I saw them. Two of them I've known a long spell. The third man runs with them from time to time."

The man sighed and put away the shell.

The fire crackled, leaping red in the night. To the staring man its flames seemed stamped forever in the brass smoothness of the final cylinder. Tiny in brass, those fireflames danced and twisted, curving in on themselves as if silently mocking the lean man. Try and find me, Abel Kinniston. You can never find me. I'm the last of the bunch and the smartest of them all. I might even be as smart as you! The man by the fire nodded thoughtfully.

"Tom Yancy," he murmured, and swallowed what was left of the coffee. It was cold and bitter. He threw the cup from him so that it bounced off a stone and rolled back against his boot. As if goaded by its touch Kinniston said harshly, "Why, damn your eyes? Why'd you do it? Didn't you know I'd come after you, one by one, until I got you all?"

His hand was a stab in the night going for the shell. His fingers crushed around it as if it held the life of the man he hated most in the world. With cold fury making a bitterness on his tongue, he opened his hand and looked down at the empty cartridge.

"I almost had it, the honest life I've wanted. It was so close, just a matter of a few miles and a few words. Now I'll never find it."

Loneliness lay frozen in his staring eyes as he rose to his feet and stood framed tall and lean against the night sky. His gaze went upward to the clouds, seeing the wedge of geese sailing low against their silver. The wild things of the land were going north with spring. The man felt an inner kinship with them. They left no mark upon the land; neither did an outlaw. They had no home, nothing to call their own other than what went with them through the clouds; neither did Abel Kinniston.

He was something of a legend in the land, this Abel Kinniston, for it had always been his habit to ride alone. He and his great appaloosa stallion were rarely seen in the trail towns or in the cities mushrooming up from the Rio Grande to the Kootenai. He followed the back trails, the narrow hoofpaths between the mountains and up along the high ridges. Sometimes he stopped at a lonely adobe shack where a sheepherder lived, to eat wheatcakes and drink coffee, or at one of the ramshackle saloons that were known only to a hard, tough breed of men, for *aguardiente* or rye whiskey.

The yellow spring blossoms of the Arizona deserts knew his lean figure in black trousers and black flannel shirt, as did the high juniper slopes of the San Juans close beside the Old Spanish Trail. There were times, when the need for action worked in his muscles, that he would swing from the saddle—it could be a boulder field along the Snake or a stand of Joshua trees below Fort Apache—and his hands would blur and his big Colt revolver buck and flame. The echoes of his shooting died away and left no trace behind him of his passing.

He was a shadow touching the Texas brasada and the moraines beyond Alder Gulch, and the instant of its touching brought a whisper of the men dead before the swiftness of his draw. Those who had never seen him scoffed a little at his name, believing it a myth; those who knew him—and these were very few—smiled tightly with the confidence of knowledge in their eyes.

Above all, he was a lonely man who spoke to animals more often than he did to people. A black bear shuffling through the timberlands of the Black Hills, a scampering brush rabbit out of a flatland hole along the Platte, a pronghorn antelope with its white tail bobbing madly as it fled across the grasslands of west Texas: these were his only confidants. The wild things and his stallion, they heard the troubled murmurs of his heart, the instinctive hungers of his blood, the deep ache of his tired muscles. And as the years fled away under the walking hooves of the palouse, Abel Kinniston became something of a wild animal himself.

He grew used to the starry sky above his head at night, to the grate of dust under his boots at an early morning camp. His food he shot and ate on the trail. When a shirt or a pair of trousers wore out, he came into a town like Dodge or Tascosa and bought a new one, riding on without doing more than paying for his purchase. In these rare appearances, he seemed like nothing more than a visiting rancher, never a cowhand. His clothes were too neat and expensive for that. There was pride in Abel Kinniston, and that pride made him face the world with his own sober estimate of Abel Kinniston plain for all to read.

A wolf howled in the breaks to the south.

The man shook himself from his dreamings. A wedge of honking geese and the muted wail of a hungry lobo, strangely musical and stirring in the silent reaches of the night, were living reminders of his own loneliness. Not for the past three years, ever since he was gunned down, had he slept on a bed and within walls. In all that time he'd eaten at a table in a house less than twenty times. The ground was his mattress, a campfire his stove.

His hand that was usually so deft and sure fumbled now as he lifted out his gun—his gaze was oddly blurred with memory, this night—to spin its cylinder and check the five brass shells. Holstering the Colt, he moved with fluid stride to his saddle and lifted out the rifle. Levering the Winchester, he eyed its load and returned it to the bucket. His bedroll lay on the pine-needled ground. His horse, a rangy palouse in blacks and grays, was tethered to a fallen log with enough rope from a maguey lariat to browse where it would.

These were nightly chores grown into habit.

Restlessness made him walk from the fire to the rim of the rock lift where he'd made his camp. Out there to the south lay the Arkansas River and the New Mexico Territory, and the stark bluffs of the Llano Estacado where for a little while he had made his stand as a small rancher. His lips twisted. Ranch life lay behind him now, as did the killings that had made him outlaw, as did all the long and lonely years which had molded him into the man he was.

Where did they bury you, Homer Morrel, and you, Toleman Ackley? On what stretch of dry prairie does your grave lie hidden, Moses Pierce?

Coldness moved with the wind past his belt buckle and settled all along his spine. The honking geese went through the clouds and faded into the darkness of the north. The hunting wolf was silent far below. The world lay quiet, as if dying all around him.

Abel Kinniston knew a lot about death. He had seen men die from the bullets in his Colt. Many times a shovel in his hand had helped to bury those whom other men had killed, too. The little trail towns he had visited had been dying while he was there, only he'd been too blind to see it. He knew their names and where the prairie wind howled now around their dry and empty buildings. Fifty Mile. Painted Post. Wilkinson. Four Trees. They were a poem of sound etched in a corner of his memory. He and others like him had helped kill them. The world has no room for its outcasts and will not give them shelter.

He felt cold and tired, suddenly.

The wind made his eyes water.

A man on a horse walking through the red dawn was the only thing that moved on the wide flatness of the high benchlands. The man sat straight in the saddle, the cantle gripping his butt. His black Stetson rode low on his forehead against the coming heat of day and he held his reins loosely as if he did not need them to guide the appaloosa stallion.

From time to time the man dismounted and stared down at the ground before him. Once he hunkered to brush fingertips across the dirt, to toss a pebble aside after studying it. Where the ground was rough and hard he rode slowly, where it lay soft and open he went at a swifter pace. From time to time he brought out a pair of field glasses—worn from overmuch use—and with them swept the land ahead. And always he rode with a hand near the smooth butt of his holstered rifle.

This was a vast and empty land through which he moved, a land as lonely as himself. In the haze of distance red sandstone ridges erupted beyond a waste of flat gravel beds and lonely clumps of palo verde. Mighty stone buttes, worn and eroded by wind and, in the days when the land was young, by rushing river waters, stood like sleeping sentinels bent against fatigue. An occasional flash of movement told him where a prairie dog had sighted him and vanished into its hole. Under the walking hooves of his horse the dry dust made tiny clouds, puffing up to fall apart and lie as undisturbed as they had been in the long centuries before his coming.

A gathering excitement rode the trickle of sweat down his spine, causing him to stand in the stirrups and send his gaze raking the vast wasteland. The sun was high overhead now, and the red rocks of the moraines flared golden as they jutted their grotesque bulks at the cloudless sky. The heat was building with every added minute of daylight. In an hour it would be a pitiless thing, baking everything along this flat stretch of plateau land. As if he did not feel the heat the man rode on, eyes fixed straight before him.

He was close to the man with the scraggly red beard. He had picked up his trail in Fort Benton and had followed his tracks down the Missouri to Three Forks and Bozeman. The old Bozeman Trail carried him into Wyoming and the fringe land bordering the Grand Tetons.

Southward through the Red Desert he had skirted the Sierra Madres and followed them past Steamboat Springs. Now he was moving along the Sawatches, a tiny mote in an utter emptiness of sun and heat and haze. His mind was as empty as these barren lands, except for the face of Red Patsy.

Abel Kinniston put his fingers to his vest pocket, touched on of the three brass shells. There was a grim satisfaction in him. For close to three years he had been following the man with the scraggly red beard.

When the heat came off the hills in the shimmering waves of a midday sun, the man reined the palouse to his near side and let him walk upward half a mile to a rock sink. A stone cup, hollowed out by wind and time and an ancient glacier, held blue water in its maw under a rock overhang which sheltered it from the sun.

The man let the horse drink before he lay flat on his belly and sipped slowly. When he was done he unstrapped a Bentley canteen from his saddle and held it under the water until it was full. The water in the sink was almost gone.

Abel Kinniston made a circuit of the *tenaja* with curious eyes. Some dozen years ago—before Custer caught Black Kettle at the Washita and smashed his power—this was a Cheyenne rendezvous. A brave would rather die than reveal its existence to a white man.

There was a pawmark in the dust below the rock.

"Only me and a coyote know about it now," said the lean man with a wry grin.

He moved up into the saddle and toed the speckled horse into a canter. Less than a score of miles from the sink there was an adobe building owned by a Mexican named Pio Pablo, who sold cheap mescal and fried tortillas. To a man who lived on the food he could shoot and the water he could find, the anticipated taste of tortillas was a sweetness to the tongue.

Pio Pablo was a fat man who panted when he walked. As a result he used his feet as seldom as possible. He had pushed a cot against an adobe wall close to the wooden bar so that he could rest more easily between the lonely visits of the riders who came out of the sunset toward his lonely shack.

He was stretching to light the oil lamp that hung on leather thongs from the ceiling when his ears caught the pound of hoofbeats. The sun was a red ball on the horizon and inside the adobe building the shadows were long and thick. Pio Pablo waved out the match and got down laboriously from the single chair he owned. He was curious as to the identity of the rider but did not honor him by going to the door.

"He will be here soon enough," he murmured, shrugging, and bent down for his big iron skillet.

Into a pool of grease he tossed half a dozen tortillas. The small iron cookstove hummed quietly with heat. Pio Pablo frowned thoughtfully, lips pursed. Abruptly he reached to the bar shelf and produced a granite coffeepot. Lonely riders meant white riders and white riders liked coffee.

The horse slid in the dust outside the shack. An instant later Pio Pablo picked up the jingle of rowels. Spanish rowels, long and cruel, which made their own special kind of music. Curious, he looked away from the coffee tin to the open doorway.

A man with red beard stubble on his heavy jaw stood on the sill, staring into the lamplit interior. Pio Pablo felt uneasiness come into his big belly. He did not like the face of this one, nor the worn look about the heavy gunbelts and their twin burdens tied low on his thighs. Men like this sometimes did not pay for the food and drink he served. They laughed at him instead and Pio Pablo, being an honest coward, laughed along with them.

The red-bearded man stepped into the room after a long, searching look. He didn't smile; Pio Pablo was sure there was no humor in him. He simply walked straight ahead and leaned his elbows on the bar.

"Tortillas and coffee," he said softly. "I'll take all you can feed me."

"It is a 'dobe dollar for both, senor."

Redbeard shrugged and put a hand in his pocket. He tossed a coin on the bar top. His pale blue eyes watched Pio Pablo reach for the big Mexican dollar and tuck it into his strained trousers.

The man ate standing at the bar, both hands moving at the same time, using knife and fork with equal ease. Pio Pablo stared, fascinated. The man was finished with two plates and starting on his third when a wagon axle creaked.

Pio Pablo did not see the redbearded man draw his gun. It was done so smoothly and so quickly that one moment the man was calmly eating tortillas, the next he was standing with his back to the bar, gun in his hand.

"Senor, senor, they are my friends," protested Pio Pablo, wringing his pudgy hands. "Many people come to my lonely bar in the night. If you are going to shoot them all—"

The redbearded man grunted and waited, gun out. When he saw the two thin Mexicans who came walking through the dying sunlight he made a little motion with his shoulders and pushed the gun back into its holster.

"Many people come here, fat one?" he asked.

"*Si*, many. *Non*, not many." Pio Pablo shrugged. "It depends. Most of them are what you call *bandido*. Not wanted in the towns. They come here to eat, to drink."

The Mexicans sidled past the gunman, eyes wide.

After a moment the redbearded man turned back to his tortillas, eating slowly. Twice he swallowed cups of steaming coffee. Nervousness made him move around the little room when he was done, examining the gourds which hung in their strings from the ceiling and the moldy cheeses lying side by side on the wooden shelf. His hand chose one. A knife came out of a pocket and cut deep. With both elbows braced on the bar and facing the open doorway which commanded a view of the night beyond it, he munched steadily.

"Fat one, you got any mescal?" he called out suddenly.

Pio Pablo turned from the far corner of the bar where he leaned with Miguel and Alonzo. "*Si*, senor. I give you a bottle."

"Do that."

The redbearded man ignored the glass to catch hold of the tall thin bottle and tilt it to his lips. Pio Pablo and his two friends watched as the fiery liquor moved down his throat. When he put the bottle on the bar it was only half full.

"Get another one, fat boy."

Pio Pablo did not like to be spoken to in such a voice, but he was not a brave man, and so he hurried as much as his bulk would permit to wipe clean another bottle and place it beside its fellow. Twice he cleared his throat before he could speak.

"It is a dollar the bottle, senor."

The redbearded man nodded carelessly, staring out the open door. Pio Pablo also looked out the door, past the man's shoulder, but all he could see was the open prairie with the blue bulk of the Ramparts in the far distance. He had seen this sight many times; he found nothing unusual about it, so he turned back to his friends. But the redbearded man continued to stare until night was a black weight across the land.

Then he swung back to the bar and leaned his forearm on it. After a little while he looked at the end of the room. "How far's Wardance, fat man?"

Pio Pablo said, "Two hundred, maybe three hundred miles, senor. To the south."

"Any landmarks to watch for?"

It was Miguel who said, "Ride for the notch in the Indian Lances. You will come to a stand of aspens. Turn left and follow the edge of the river."

Pio Pablo would have liked to ask questions but the face of the redbearded one was cold and hard. It was the face of a killer, he knew. Pio Pablo had seen a lot of such faces come and go. The less a man had to do with them the longer he would live. Pio Pablo shrugged and began to chat once more with Miguel and Alonzo.

Twice during the next hour men rode in off the flats, cowhands from the ranches half a dozen miles to the eastward along the Rio Grande, before it began its twist down into New Mexico and Texas. As each horse scattered gravel in its canter the redbearded man tensed, but he did not lift again the heavy gun at his thigh. Apparently the mescal was soothing the open wound of his nerves; Pio Pablo hoped it was, fervently, with little whispered prayers to the Madonna. There was thick dust on the red one's vest and shirt, he had ridden far, he was probably tired and not inclined to quarrel. Or so Pio Pablo hoped.

The wind shifted over the Lances, chill with remembered winter.

On the wings of that norther, another horse came through the darkness. Its hoofbeats made faint and muted music to the ears listening in the little adobe shack. There was a jingle of ringbits and the creak of saddle leather. The redbeard turned from his bottle to stare with narrowed eyes at the open doorway, then swung back to stand with hunched shoulders, both hands cupping the bottle, staring blindly at the wall over the little stove.

A bootfall crunched pebbles. A man came and stood in the doorway with his clothes worn and dusty and the look of the far traveler about his hard brown face. He wore his Stetson low on his forehead, tilted forward just above his eyes. Memory touched Pio Pablo as he came down the bar, smiling a welcome.

"*Buenos noches*, senor. You would like a little mescal?"

The stranger did not answer; he was looking at the redheaded man and Pio Pablo shivered when he saw the threat of death glinting in his eyes. The silence stretched on. It touched the red one, made him look up suddenly and angle his head around. Like that he stood frozen with his mouth a little open.

The dusty rider said, "Hello, Patsy."

Red Patsy whispered, "Oh, God. . . ."

"You didn't kill me, you and Dutch Korman and Tom Yancy. You had a fair chance at me. You hit me, too. I carry the scars of your bullets in my chest and hip and arm. I almost died, Patsy."

The wind moaned outside the shack and the flame of the oil lamp danced in answer to its song. Shadows shifted and quivered in the room. Miguel and Alonzo were very quiet. The two white ranch hands lifted their drinks and moved backward into the darker shadows, where they stood watching.

"You can try again, Patsy. Any time. I'll wait."

Pio Pablo shivered. He had thought the redheaded man was *muy duro*—a very tough man—but the dusty stranger was cold fire. Again memory stirred. He knew this man with the worn clothes and the very clean gunbelt; somewhere he'd seen that bronze face, but he could not remember his name.

Red Patsy was swinging slowly so as to put his back to the bar. His lips were trembling and he had grown very pale.

The stranger said, "This time it won't be from ambush and I don't have any money on me for you to steal. But if you ever killed a man, kill me now. Because if you don't, you'll never get the chance again."

"Kinniston, listen—"

A man exhaled sharply in the shadows. Pio Pablo found his memory coming with a rush, and now he remembered all the times he had seen this dusty man and especially the day Moses Pierce tried to beat his gunhand and failed; for the space of a single second it was like the old days, back in Texas. He put his hands on the bar and held them still by sheer will. Sweat stood in beads on his face, though he was shivering.

Laughter drifted from Abel Kinniston. Like a tangible thing it flicked the redheaded man and straightened him.

Red Patsy moved a shoulder. His gun was in his hand, lifting upward from the holster. Before the long barrel could clear the leather Kinniston fired three times. His bullets were long nails pinning the redheaded man back against the bar where he hung, head forward on his chest, legs rigid, dead on his feet. He was a long moment like that before he slumped to the hard dirt floor.

A man said from the shadows, "I didn't even see him draw." His words faded into a silence broken by the creak of dusty boot leather as Abel Kinniston knelt and put his hands to the body of Red Patsy.

From an inside pocket of his coat he brought out an envelope and stared at it curiously. He had not known that Red Patsy could read. There was a postal stamp on the envelope and a date. Wardance, N. Mex. and the date was December 12, 1879.

The years of his trailing had put an instinct in Abel Kinniston. His nostrils flared and his eyes narrowed. Eagerly he opened the envelope, found part of a torn letter inside.

. . . .come down to Wardance and join your old friends. Dutch says hello, and wants me to say that you can make yourself a bundle here if you want it. The place is open for the taking. All a man needs is a fast gun and a little guts. You have both, so why not. . . .

It was enough. Kinniston closed his fist, crumpling the letter. He didn't need to have the rest of the writing to know who had sent it. He went through the pockets of the worn, dusty pants, taking out some folded bills and loose change, which he put on the counter.

"The body's worth five thousand American dollars, Pio," he said softly. "Take it in to Cripple Creek and claim the reward." His gesture indicated the loose change and crumpled bills. "That'll pay for his food and drinks."

Pio Pablo swallowed. "You remember Pio Pablo, *si*?"

The dusty man let the corner of his lips twitch. The Mexican took it for a smile. "Could I ever forget it? The Morrels and Moses Pierce and dusty, dirty little Sundown, where I grew up. I've been trying for a dozen years to forget Sundown. Don't remind me of it."

His boot touched the dead man on the floor. He drew back and frowned. "Cook me up some tortillas. I'll eat them on the trail. And let me have a bottle of mescal. I have a long ride ahead of me."

Only Pio Pablo moved, bustling around the little stove. He said conversationally, "*El muerto* was riding for Wardance."

Abel Kinniston nodded. When the Mexican was done with his cooking he put the tortillas in a piece of cloth and wrapped it over three times. He handed a bottle to Kinniston, but Kinniston did not take it. His hand was fumbling in a vest pocket.

His hand lifted out an empty cartridge shell. Idly he turned it over and over, as if seeing it for the first time. Pio Pablo felt his eyes drawn and held by that tiny cylinder. When Kinniston made a pouring motion with it, as if spilling the lifeblood of a man, Pio Pablo sighed thickly.

Kinniston let the shell go. It hit the redheaded man on his bloody shirt, and went rolling down his belly to his hip and off his thigh onto the floor. It came to rest against a dirty boot.

"*Muy Gracias*," whispered Kinniston, reaching for the bottle.

Then he was gone and the fading hoofbeats of a tired horse made echo to the rising murmur of the wind. For several minutes there was no movement in the adobe trail house. Then one of the cowhands came from the darkness and stood staring down at the dead man.

"Red Patsy," he said. "I've heard plenty about him. I always thought he was a fast gun."

His companion said softly, "Fast, fast. The other one was Kinniston, you fool. Didn't you hear him?"

Manuel made the Sign of the Cross.

chapter 2

The Kid rode a paint horse straight across the grasslands. Satisfaction with life and with his place in it made a gentle warmth behind his shellbelts. He was drawing gunman wages from the big Fencepost ranch; he was known and respected—even feared—in the town of Wardance; and he was in love with blond Fay Mercer. Life was sweet to the taste this morning and the Kid savored it to the full.

It took him an hour to get off Fencepost holdings and onto Triangle graze. He went at a steady canter which the paint could hold all day if necessary. When they moved past the big rock that marked part of the property line, the Kid tightened his lazy slouch and sat straighter in the kak. Triangle was Mercer territory, and you never knew with the shiftless Mercers. The old man or Benjie might be somewhere around with a rifle handy to the reach. Neither of them had much use for the Kid.

For another thirty minutes he was the only moving thing on stretch of grama grass. Then he came in sight of three steers browsing. The Kid reached for his Winchester. Mister Young had told him to shoot anything not human when he saw it moving on Triangle graze. Mister Young did not like the Mercers; he wanted their land and hoped to scare them into moving off it.

The Kid fired three times. When he reined the paint onward, the three steers lay stiff on the ground. Too bad, the Kid reflected with a wry grin; those animals would make plenty of good thick steaks. The Kid liked steaks. Maybe he could come back with a wagon and get them, if Mister Young agreed. Hell, no sense letting good food rot.

He circled wide to avoid the ramshackle Triangle ranch house; no need to get himself shot. His job was in the nature of a nuisance gun, to keep the Mercers off balance and angry. The paint topped a little ridge and the Kid drew him up to let him blow, while his eyes ran the length of Butterwood Creek.

A bay horse was down there near the creek, standing hipshot with its long tail switching flies. There were two spots of color on the ground close by its hooves, something yellow and something blue. The Kid grinned. That Fay Mercer was sure a clean one. He'd heard it rumored she took baths every day. Now he had the proof before him.

The willow trees were thick around this section of the creek where it went wide to form a small pool. It hid the girl who swam so that the Kid could see her only as an occasional flash of white skin. He chuckled. Life sure was good to him these days. His toe nudged the paint down the slope.

He swung groundward a dozen feet from the bay. The yellow shirtwaist and blue levis caught his glance, then he was walking past them through the stand of willows to the creek bank.

"Hey, anybody around?" he called.

The girl with the long yellow hair whirled in the water, crying out, letting herself sink down until only her pert face was above the surface. Her hair floated a moment, spread out on the ripples to form a golden fan, before it sank out of sight. The Kid was silent in sheer awe. He'd give anything to be able to run his palms over that blonde mane.

"Bobby, you scat," the girl yelled angrily.

"No need to rile yourself," he told her. Too bad she'd muddied up the water so much, swimming like she had. He grinned toothily. "Come on out. We'll sit and talk a mite."

"You skidaddle, Bobby Cranford! If Pop or Benjie show up—"

The Kid made a wry face. He did not like his given name. To him it smacked of something childish. He said, "They won't. Come up here on the bank. I've been thinking about you a lot lately."

She did not answer but seemed to shrink in the water even more. The Kid eyed her pretty face with its sullen pout that made her red lips look riper, larger. Anger swept into his throat with the speed of a flash flood.

"You don't come out, you'll be sorry," he shouted.

"Be sorry if I do," she yelled back.

The Kid grinned and moved away from the bank. The girl would think he was going, he knew; he laughed silently to himself, stepping past the shirtwaist and levis to his horse. He had one foot in the stirrup when he pretended to see her clothes for the first time. Very carefully he walked over to them, bent and lifted them into a hand.

"Well now," he said, loud enough for Fay Mercer to hear. "What do you know? Somebody went an' lost their duds. A shame, a shame. Reckon I'll have to bring 'em in to Marshal Kesselring for his lost and found department."

"Bobby Cranford, if you dare!"

"'Course if I found out who they belonged to, if someone was to walk right up to me this minute and claim them, I'd have to give them back to whoever it was. No questions asked, neither."

He looked at the girl in the water and chuckled. She sure was pretty when she was riled. Sparks burst in her blue eyes. Those pouting lips were firmed almost to a thin line. In her excitement she was half standing; when she saw him focus his stare she flushed and sank back into the muddied water.

"Enough is enough," she yelled.

"The lady's right. Let go her clothes."

The Kid was having so much fun that he almost didn't hear the quiet voice. When it came through to him, he let the clothes go and went for his gun even while he was turning on a bootheel.

A dusty man sat the saddle of an appaloosa, black hat forward almost to his eyes. There was a Frontier model Colt in his hand aimed at the Kid's beltbuckle. The barrel did not waver. The Kid took his hand away from his gunbutt.

The Kid sneered. "Put up your gun and go for it when my back isn't turned, stranger."

"Go fork your kak and hightail out of here."

"I said—"

"I heard what you said. Now you listen and you listen good, son. Haul butt out. *Muy pronto*. You savvy?"

The Kid flushed and stammered. He sought to sneer again but something about those cold gray eyes held him paralyzed. They were sad eyes but they looked deep down inside him, touching wellsprings the Kid thought he'd lost forever: his early fear of the dark, the time he'd fallen from that treelimb and broken a leg, the runaway horse when he was ten and astride it, hanging on by sheer dumb luck. His tongue came out to moisten his lips but it was bone dry. His throat was dry, too. He couldn't even swallow.

He didn't know what was the matter with him. No coward, he'd already shot three men in Main Street gunfights. His blood ought not to freeze like this, just looking in a man's face. The Kid was fascinated by what he could read in the eyes that ate at him.

"Get going," said the dusty rider, and jerked his head.

The Kid noticed that he'd put his Colt back into his holster and he was surprised, for the Kid hadn't seen him do it though he'd been looking at him all the time. Maybe he was waiting for the Kid to start the play. Something deep within the Kid shied from that notion. He walked toward the paint horse a little faster.

The Kid rode off without looking back.

Abel Kinniston waited until the Kid topped the far ridge and started down the other side before he nudged the palouse to a walk. He skirted the creek pool and moved past the bay mare and straight ahead along the creek bank.

"Hey! You!" yelled the girl. "Wait up, will you?"

Kinniston could hear splashing sounds. After a moment the voice said, "Don't you turn around now, mister." He sat quietly until he heard bare feet running through the grass toward him. Then she was standing beside his off stirrup, staring up with wide blue eyes, tucking a yellow shirtwaist over wet flesh into tight levis.

"What'd you do to him?" she asked breathlessly.

"Do? Nothing"

"That's what I mean. You didn't curse or shoot but you sure scared poor Bobby Cranford witless. He's supposed to be a hardcase."

"Bobby Cranford?"

"Awww, everybody 'round here calls him The Kid, 'cept me. I tease him. He hates his name. But he's a bad one just the same."

"A gunfighter, you mean."

The shirtwaist was damp now and clinging to her firm young breasts. Kinniston wondered if she knew the buttons were done up lopsided. She was a pretty thing with a pixie face and faintly slanted blue eyes with long yellow lashes. Slim inside a black leather belt, her hips made curving mounds in the taut levis.

"Well sure, a gunfighter. A Fencepost man."

"You don't like Fencepost," he stated flatly.

"I hate their guts," she lashed out. "They shoot our cattle, they gang up on Benjie in a fistfight three, four to one when he rides into town for supplies, they—" Her shoulder lifted as she eyed him with her head tilted sideways, wrinkling up her nose and narrowing her eyes against the afternoon sun. "No sense telling you our troubles, is there?"

His hand lifted the reins. "I'll be riding on, ma'am." His hand touched the brim of the dusty black Stetson.

"Is there, mister?" she repeated.

"Is there what?"

"Any sense telling you Triangle's troubles?"

His mouth twitched. He shook his head. "No sense."

"You weren't afraid of Bobby."

Surprise made him look at her more sharply, so that he could read her expression as she pressed him with words. "What I mean is, he's a badman."

"He thinks he's a badman," he told her gently.

"Thinks or is, he has plenty of folks believing the way he does around here. Men in Wardance and on the ranches. You now, you didn't buckle. You made him buckle. Without doing anything at all, far's I could see."

Kinniston shifted his rump against the cantle. There was no way to tell a girl about all the things a man could learn in eleven, twelve years along the narrow trails from El Paso north into Milk River country. Abel Kinniston could see into a man with his eyes but there was no way to explain how he did it. The gift was with him, like his gunhand. And so he only looked a little puzzled and lifted the reins again.

The blond girl put a hand on his stirrup leather, clinging to it. She smiled up at him, crinkling her nose again. "You don't talk much, do you mister? You got a name? Where you headed?" She paused a moment to let him answer but when he was silent she laughed a little, almost under her breath, and said, "My turn to cook supper, so it'll be good tonight. You come on up to the house and meet Pop and Benjie. I'd like them to see you, hear you tell what it is you did to scare Bobby so."

He shook his head soberly, making his voice flat as he said, "I'd be obliged if you stood aside, ma'am."

Her pert face grew rebellious. "I won't and you can't make me." Her hand tightened its grip on the black leather. Way her head was tilted up at him with her eyes slanted against the sun and her mouth pouting like that put an urge in him to lean over to kiss her, just to see her jump back. Soon as she let go, he'd toe the spotted horse into a canter.

Kinniston tried to make the palouse shy to one side by tightening his knees but the girl kept following him. Now she was smiling flirtatiously, her pert nose wrinkling a little.

"Come on, mister. Tell me. How'd you spook

Bobby so easily?"

"He knew I'd kill him if he went for his gun."

She considered that, lifting a hand to put aside a strand of the thick yellow hair windblown across her face. "How did he know that?"

"I don't know. He did. A lot of men can see something in my eyes, way I see it in theirs."

The girl shook her head back and forth without moving her gaze from his face. "I don't understand. I guess I never will. My offer of that home cooking still goes."

Something like fright blossomed in Kinniston. He was a lonely man but he enjoyed his loneliness, for it left him beholden to no one. Suspicion and mistrust made him shy away from this pretty girl; he knew he was like a wild animal veering from the overtures of a human trying to make friends. Still, a man can live too much alone, and man is something better than an animal. His left hand tightened on the worn reins.

"Obliged, ma'am. Some other time."

"No. Now! I'll ride with you."

Her laughter was soft, infectious. She was laughing with him as if she could sense the shyness and the emptiness below his gray eyes and hard face, as if with her laughter she might lure out that animal wariness and soothe it into submission. Her hand touched his knee and he thought her palm was very warm.

"Please? I'll make dumplings and a pie—Bud picked elderberries yesterday—and there's two dead chickens in the springhouse just achin' to be fried."

Kinniston sighed. Here it was again, the way it had been a few other times in his past. He hated himself for it but he had to kill this friendliness. His elbow rested on the saddlehorn as he leaned down to her.

"Look, ma'am. You don't know me or my name,

who I am or my reputation. If I came to eat at your house and a lawman was to walk in your front door and recognize me, there'd be gunplay. I'd be forced to kill him. I got two men yet to kill, ma'am. After that, why—maybe nothing will matter very much to me any more. But right now. . . ."

His words trailed off. Kinniston knew he was not getting through to her at all. Her blue eyes were dancing in mischief and her mouth was trying to suppress laughter. She said, "You think you're a badman too, just like Bobby."

Exasperation made him scowl. "Look, little girl. My name is Abel Kinniston." He waited, watching her merry eyes, but she only nodded and said, "That's a very pretty name. I like it." And then she doubled over with laughter, her hands clinging to her middle where the levis were so tight. She staggered a little, laughing so hard, and her head bumped Kinniston's leg. Wonderingly he looked down at her.

"You men," she said at last, wiping her eyes with the heel of a palm. "You think you're all so wicked. One is worse than the other." Her lips firmed as she became serious. "I'm inviting you to my home, Abel Kinniston—and I won't take any nonsense about your being too wicked to eat at the same table with me."

"Ma'am, I've told you I can't. That settles it."

Her eyes looked at him slyly. "Maybe Bobby Cranford is waiting to annoy me again, somewhere beyond the ridge. If anything happened to me, it'd be your fault."

Kinniston scowled. It had been so long since he had sat to table with a woman, he could not remember the last time. He had a horror of house walls, of floors and ceilings; he supposed it had something to do with the gunfight with Roy Torrance and his two brothers, back in Three Wells, when they trapped him in a town house and damn near finished him off between them.

He shifted his butt in the kak, uneasy against the stare of her blue eyes and the amused curl of her mouth. He had no real reason not to go with her but he was a loner, a timber wolf afraid of humankind, a man who had run alone for almost all his life. He did not want to break the habit now, so close to Wardance.

He thought of Bobby Cranford. Fool kid! Just because his hand moved a little faster than most folks, he had taken a fancy to himself. Thinking of the Kid made him realize that this girl was a neighbor to the men in Wardance and might know Dutch Korman or Tom Yancey. He cleared his throat.

"Might be the Kid will double back," he said slowly. "I could ride a spell with you."

"Just in case?" she asked soberly.

"Just in case." He nodded.

She let out a whoop and ran to the bay mare. Kinniston watched her run, annoyed at himself and at the girl. She ought to be paddled properly on that rounded butt where the levis were so taut. Fried chicken and dumplings, though. His mouth could not remember the sweet taste of chicken with dumplings. He would play his cards right, eat the meal she cooked and be off before moon-up.

The bay mare came dancing up. "I'm Fay Mercer," she told him, letting the mare move out in front, the big palouse following at its hip. "My Pop owns Triangle, such as it is."

"Good land," he murmured, using his eyes, running them away from the ridge they were mounting, across the creek and over the expanding grasslands. "Your stock can grow real fat here."

"You know ranching?"

"A little."

"Hand or foreman?"

"I owned a spread east of the Pecos."

Her eyes slid sideways. "You sell out?"

When he shook his head the girl chuckled. "Tell me to mind my own business. You might as well. You make it pretty plain."

Kinniston fought his tongue and lost. "Three men shot me from an arroyo. I almost died. Would have if an old Navajo hadn't found me, took me to his hogan, doctored me up for eight weeks."

She waited patiently. They were moving stirrup to stirrup across a grassy flat with the breeze stirring the blue grama, making it sway beneath the fetlocks of their horses. Memory was coming back to the man, making him wince against the red pain of those blurred days when death sat waiting in the hogan doorway.

"You ever hear of Homer Morrel? Thought not. You're too young. The old man—Old Homer, that is—was walking terror. He feuded with the Tollivers, Homer did, about eleven, twelve years ago, over Pecos River way. The trouble grew out of a herd of cattle, mavericks we called them, since they were no brand and belonged to any man willing to move into the brush country for them.

"My dad was foreman for Lucius Tolliver. I was fifteen, sixteen then and fancied myself just about the way the Kid fancies himself. I was brash and sassy. I knew horses and I was fast with a gun. Some of it came natural, the rest was hard work. Sweat and strain in that damn New Mexico sun until I sometimes couldn't lift my arms. Both arms. One gun wasn't enough. I had to wear two."

He caught the sideways glance of her eyes and smiled tightly. "I got a little sense in the years between. One gun kills a man just as dead as two.

"Anyway, Old Homer claimed a herd of slicks we'd flushed from the river flats belonged to him. The Tolliver Box T was on their flanks but Homer Morrel said we'd stole them. He sent a gun crew to a Tolliver trail herd campfire. There was an argument. Three Tolliver men died before it was ended. One of those three men was my father. Moses Pierce—old Homer's segundo and the fastest gun in those parts—was the ramrod for that gun crew. It was his bullet did my dad in.

"I rode into town next day and looked up Moses. He laughed when he heard I was hunting him. He came out of the saloon—the Palace, it was called. I can still see him walking through the dust, coming at me. I killed him. Before I got out of town I had to kill another Morrel rider. The feud was on then.

"It lasted three years. Old Homer hired gunmen. We didn't bother to hire anybody. I was a headstrong young fool. It went to me head that I was so good with a Colt I could go against anybody Homer Morrell could find to throw at me. All told I killed eleven men in gunfights. One of these men was Toleman Ackley. Some folks said he was faster than Wes Hardin. I wouldn't know. I've never met Hardin.

"I was drawing killer wages. I put nearly every cent in a bank in Three Wells. When the feud was over—both crews got together in a back trail town one afternoon and shot it out to a finish, and we had Old Homer and Morrel and Lucius Tolliver with us—both Morrel and Tolliver were dead. Only womenfolk were left. Norma Jean Tolliver sold her interests and went back to New Orleans. Nancy Morrel sold out too but she died before she could reach California.

"All I got out of the fighting was a reputation and

a few thousand dollars in a cowtown bank. I was young and cocky. I thought I was sitting on top of the world. Wasn't I the Tolliver gun, the only one out of both outfits who was in at the start and at the finish? The others were dead or had been run off."

They were cantering across a ridge speckled with creosote bushes. In the distance Kinniston made out the brown logwork of a ranch house and the rails of a corral unbalancing it to one side. There were some sheds, rickety things he judged them at first glance, and a well between them.

"Triangle," said Fay with a deadness in her voice.

Kinniston let her go down the ridge trail first, knowing she would turn even before she did to look at him in that quiet way she had. "And after that? After Norma Jean Tolliver sold out and went back to New Orleans, what did you do then?"

"I hired out to kill men."

If he expected her pert features to show shock, he was disappointed. Almost casually she said, "You weren't even twenty." After a time she spoke again. "Did you kill many men?"

"Enough."

"It was all you knew how to do."

"Why no," Kinniston said, a little surprised. "I knew ranching. I could have worked my guts out over a branding fire or riding up the Chisholm with the herds. I could earn more money with a gun." His laughter was brittle. "It was a lot easier work. Then I killed one man too many, I suppose. They made me an outlaw."

The girl reined up in sheer surprise. "After so many gunfights? I mean, I should think—" She looked flustered.

"They were all fair fights. They didn't call Abel Kinniston in to shoot some poor dirt farmer. The men I was asked to bring down were hired guns themselves. Everybody knew it when we hooked up on some main drag. It was done out in the open, face to face. The faster hand won. It was like a game. I helped build a lot of spreads in those early days, spreads I wouldn't dare ride over now for fear of getting a bullet in the back."

"They're afraid of you, is that it? You cleared out the bad element for a price, like a town marshal."

His mouth twisted at a corner. "A town marshal works by the law. Men like me live by their own laws, their own code. A ranch owner was running into trouble from some wildcat outfit, let's say. The wildcat outfit had hired a gun to frighten opposition. The honest man sent for me, paid me a thousand dollars to rid him of the gunman. I did my job, collected my wages, and rode on."

"It doesn't seem fair," she protested.

"My eyes were wide open. I got nobody to blame but myself. I balanced the scale, then made my choice."

The girl held her bay mare to a slow walk. "And when they made you an outlaw?"

"I forgot my name, used the money I had on me to buy a two-bit ranch in the Sand Hills country and worked hard to make it stick. I did make it stick, too, for a few years." He couldn't help the pride that ran on his tongue. "Then there was an amnesty. All outlaws could turn honest. All a man needed do was make restitution of sorts. If I was a train robber I could turn in my loot. I was a killer. Not much I could do except turn in my gun, was there?"

"N-no, I guess not."

"I wrote the governor, asked him about my case, using my false name. I suppose he knew it was me—he was no fool, that man. He wrote back suggesting I hand over the blood money I'd earned over the years. Do that and he'd sign me a full pardon with his own hand."

He was not used to talking so much. His throat was dry and sore. Sometimes he went three, four days in the saddle without making a sound. His hand went to the big Bentley canteen, unscrewing its cap, tilting it to his mouth. He wiped the black flannel shirtsleeve across his lips.

"So I went and got the blood money, from banks in El Paso and Three Wells, in Baxter Springs and in San Antone. Some bills I'd hidden away in coffee tins. I dug them up. I carried it all with me in my saddlebags. Nearly forty thousand dollars.

"When I was some miles outside Sante Fe I fell out of the saddle with three bullets in me. The money was in my saddlebags waiting to be taken. I lay on the ground and heard them talking. One wanted to put his gun to my head. The others talked him out of it. Somebody might come along any minute and find them. They grabbed my saddlebags and ran."

"And the Indian found you."

"Three years ago, all this happened. I've been riding ever since, hunting those men. I found one of them. He's dead."

"And the others?"

His hand touched his shirt pocket where a rumpled envelope lay folded. "I'm playing a hunch they're in Wardance."

"Why, Wardance's only ten miles from here!"

"I figured that. I was riding there when I saw the Kid peekin' at you."

Excitement made her squirm. "What're their names? The men you're after? Maybe I know them."

"Dutch Korman. Tom Yancey."

Disappointment made her pout. "I was hoping I could help you. I've never heard of either of them. But maybe Pop has, or Benjie."

They came into the dusty emptiness of the Triangle yard at a slow walk. Kinniston moved his gaze from the broken porch steps to the front door where it sagged on one hinge. The girl flushed and would not meet his eyes as she slipped from the saddle, but she walked with her spine straight and her blond head high.

"You can wash up around back," she told him, looking out across the land. The wind came up and blew around her, sending the long yellow hair dancing over her shoulders and across her face.

"Thank you," Kinniston said solemnly. "I'm obliged."

Her glance sought him out as he stepped from the stirrup. She kicked at a clod of dirt with a worn boot. "Pop isn't much of a handyman, I guess. Neither's Benjie."

"Where'd you say that wash-up tin was?"

She smiled faintly, her eyes almost tender as they lingered on his brown face. "Come on, mister. I'll show you." She brought water from the well bucket and filled the tin basin that rested on a wooden bench behind the house. For a long moment she watched him throw water over his face and in his ears before she ran into the house. She came back with a bar of soap and a clean towel.

"You can do a better job with these. I haven't got much manners, I suppose. Living here, I never get to see a stranger." She giggled. "I got nobody to practice manners on, I mean."

When he was clean and was running a comb through his thick black hair, Fay said, "You aren't bad-looking, mister. There's kind of a lonesome air about you, but your features are real good." She added hastily, "But I guess you don't give a hoot about that."

Kinniston smiled with a twist of his lips. "I've been lonely the way a gray wolf is lonely. He doesn't know any other life but running by himself."

"A wolf can take a mate and have cubs."

"His mate's a wolf too, ma'am."

She said suddenly, "Pop could use a good hand. Though I guess we couldn't pay much wages."

He handed back the towel and the soap. "You usually kill the chickens you eat?"

"What? Oh! We keep them in the near shed."

Fay watched his fluid walk, saw his hand go out to the ax and bring it loose with a quick movement of the arm from the tree stump into which Benjie had embedded it. He went on toward the shed without pausing. She wanted to stay and watch; she could hardly get her fill of looking at him. Somehow it seemed unladylike to stand and stare, though. Pop was always telling her to be a lady, but when she pressed him about details he knew as little on the subject as she did.

Her mother had died a long time ago—all Fay could remember was long hair bent above her bed and a gentle voice singing her to sleep—and Pop had tried to be a father and a mother. Pop did his best. She guessed he didn't have very good material to work with, in her. Or maybe it was because she'd never cared very much, before now, about being a lady.

She firmed her lips, thinking, Piffle! I've got to get him out of my head. If I don't, Pop and Benjie will be here for their dinner and it won't be ready. She marched herself firmly up the creaking porch steps and into the kitchen. Fay was relieved to see that Benjie'd put firewood in the scuttle. She would have dreaded going out and chopping kindling with the tall man there to watch. A real lady never chopped her own firewood, she'd bet; and suddenly, desperately, she wanted Abel Kinniston to look on her as a lady.

The fire was making a gentle crackle and there was grease in the iron skillet when he came to the back door, two plucked chickens in his left hand. When he caught her eye he moved his head a little. "Wagon coming. You folks own a wagon?"

The girl nodded. "You've got good ears, mister. There's a dry hub to that wagon I'm always telling Pop to oil. We got no oil, though." She took the chickens from his hand and walked to the sink, where a wooden tub of water lay. A moment she examined the fowls before glancing at him, saying, "You did a good job. They're real clean. You that good at other chores?"

He was gone from the doorway, she saw; moving toward it, she saw him in the yard, just waiting, watching the wagon come around the edge of the barn.

Pop reined in and sat with his mouth open, staring at the stranger. Benjie stood up, fists clenched. There was a rifle under the seat and Fay was surprised that Benjie didn't reach for it; then she looked at Kinniston and saw him the way Benjie would see him, lean and deadly. Fright touched her with a cold spasm.

"Pop, Benjie—he's a friend!"

She ran down the broken steps to stand beside him. Pop climbed out of the wagon slowly. Fay looked at Kinniston, trying to read the brown face that was so hard and flat, wondering how he would see this little man who was her father. Could he tell how the years had beaten him into subjection, rounding off his shoulders and giving him the limp where a cow had kicked him? Was he able to know the heartbreak of the dry years and the deep terror of no food, no money? As Pop came through the dust of the little yard her heart swelled in sympathy for the worn hands, the seamed face, the haggard eyes.

"I was swimming in the creek when Bobby Cranford started peeking at me. This man scared him off."

"Doggone, girl," said Pop plaintively. "I've told you not to go down there when one of us menfolk wasn't in callin' distance." He held out his hand. "I'm mighty obliged, stranger."

Benjie had been easing the grain sacks from the buckboard; he turned now and looked long at Kinniston. He was tall and heavy in the chest and his hands, like Pop's, were rough with callus. Benjie was a hard worker, with no nonsense about him, Fay knew. There were times when she felt sorry for him and the tattered, patched clothes he had to wear—no fifteen-dollar neckerchiefs and hundred-dollar spurs, the kind Bobby Cranford owned, for him—and tried to make it up by slipping him a little extra food from her own plate.

Benjie said, "He scared the Kid? And there wasn't a gunfight?" His direct gaze told Kinniston he knew he was a gunfighter and that when anybody who carried a gun at his thigh crossed the Kid, bullets flew.

"There wasn't any fight. No need for one."

It was the first time Kinniston had spoken, the first time Fay Mercer had really caught the deadly flatness of his voice when he talked to a man. When he'd been talking to Cranford, she'd been crouched in the water, she recalled, not able to hear very well.

"I don't understand," said Benjie, pressing it, fully turned from the old wagon. "The Kid thinks he's a fast gun. You don't look like any slouch, either."

Pop said, "Shut your yap, Benjie."

Fay said, "I saw it, Benjie, I tell you. Mister Kinniston had the drop on Bobby, then he put his gun back into his holster and waited. Bobby just looked at him, got a kind of sickly white, got on his horse and rode off."

"Well," said Benjie, fumbling for another sack.

Pop squinted against the dying sun. "You mebbe lookin' fer work, mister?"

"I already asked him. He's not. He's just staying for supper, then moving on." She added, unable to quell the bitterness on her tongue, "Anyhow, what kind of money could we pay him?"

"Fencepost could pay him," Benjie muttered, hauling leather traces toward the open barn door. He stopped and looked at Kinniston. "Fencepost would pay you plenty to get us out of here. Might even go as high as a hundred dollars for the job."

Kinniston said quietly. "My fees start around a thousand."

Benjie almost dropped the horse gear. Fay tugged at Kinniston then, turning him and her father toward the porch steps. She felt the involuntary movement by which he tried to free his elbow and she thought, a wild animal would be like this, nervous and alert against the restriction of a human hand. For some reason she couldn't put a finger to, she liked this quality of Abel Kinniston. She smiled up at him, saw his features soften slightly.

"Come along. Please?"

He went with her at an angling walk that kept the barn to his left. He thinks Benjie's got a gun in there and might try to use it, she told herself. The idea made her want to laugh and cry at the same time. Slightly flustered, she pushed at Pop, making him take the lead.

"Benjie, come on," she called, and waited until he was walking toward them with his long arms swinging at his sides before she joined Kinniston.

"You men go talk," she told them, moving toward the plucked chickens in the tub of water. "I've got cooking to do."

She knew Pop would head for the crock in which he kept his pipe tobacco, then turn and look around the room helplessly. Fay called, "Pipe's on the mantel with the matches." Her hands busied themselves in the water, listening with a corner of her mind to the sounds in the next room. Pop would be lighting his pipe now, puffing lustily, eyes half closed in enjoyment. After that he always sat in the old rocker—the creak of wood made her smile tenderly—and crossed his legs.

"Don't see many strangers 'round these parts, mister."

"Leastwise not on Triangle land," Benjie added. Her brother would be standing at the front door, looking out toward the grama grass in the distant fields, sober and serious. "Fencepost gets the strangers, the men with the guns tied low."

Fay writhed in embarrassment. The way they talked to him, as if he were some raw young boy like Bobby Cranford! She wanted to put her tongue into the talk, to order Pop and Benjie to mind their manners. Instead she put an extra lick of grease on the chickens, slapping it down in vexation, and shoved the pan into the oven of the big hayburner stove. Then she put her hands to her cheeks and found them hot. Well, no wonder, the way a girl had to listen to her menfolks carry on sometimes.

"You riding to Fencepost?" asked Benjie bluntly.

"Riding into Wardance."

"To get a job?"

"To kill two men."

Pop was choking on his pipe. Even Benjie was silent. Fay could picture him standing in the doorway dumbly staring at Kinniston. Then she heard him give a snorting kind of laugh.

"At least you're honest. Who are they?"

"Dutch Korman. Tom Yancey. You know them?"
"Never heard of either of them."

"Dutch is a mean bastard with shaggy yellow hair. Always wears two guns. And he's fast with them. Fast as I am, maybe. I aim to find out." There was silence for as long as it took Fay to tiptoe across the kitchen floor and peer around the hanging curtain in the doorway of the living room. Then Kinniston said, "Yancey is the slick one. Looks like—and is—a gambler. Tall and thin. Too smart to be openly mean like Korman. Black hair, black eyes. Long fingers. Has a habit of whistling to himself when he's playing stud poker."

Pop looked at Benjie, then shook his head. "You don't ring no bells with me, mister. You, Benjie?"

"Don't know anybody like that. Tell you the truth, we don't know too many folks in Wardance, come to think of it. Never go into town 'cept to buy flour and bacon."

There was no disappointment on the hard brown face, Fay saw; there was no emotion at all. It made Fay want to shake him, remembering what those men had done to him. He was standing close beside the mantel—where no bullet can come at him from behind, she thought suddenly—with his head bowed a little as if in deep thought. A thumb was hooked into the sagging shellbelt. He gave the appearance of a man lost in thought, but Fay knew the faintest sound would make him come alive with the wolf life in his gray eyes and death sitting on his gunhand. He fascinated her as might a handsome puma which had attached itself to her; she looked on him as both a challenge to her womanhood and a threat to her safety.

"I'll try in Wardance, anyhow," he said softly, as if he were talking to himself. "It won't harm to have a look around."

Pop stirred, taking his pipe from his mouth. "Look now, mister. If you want to stay here, make it your home, that is, we'd be pleased to have you. While you look around, I mean."

Kinniston smiled and once more Fay was struck by the change that came over his features; they softened and grew friendly as if a veil had been torn away. "I'm obliged, but I'll move on after supper. Best that way."

"Law after you?" asked Benjie abruptly. "Not that I give a good damn, you understand, the law being what it is around Wardance. It's just that if we knew for sure we could keep our mouths shut."

"We'll keep 'em shut regardless," growled Pop, knocking dottle from the pipebowl. "Triangle's got no friends to blab to, anyhow."

Kinniston shifted weight. "I won't be a burden to any man. You tell folks whatever they want to know about me."

Pop said, "We'll tell nothing to nobody."

There was small talk after that, with Kinniston withdrawing into his shell again. Words came hard to his tongue, even when Fay could see he wanted to speak freely about grazeland and how the white-faced Herefords were pushing the tough longhorns into oblivion. The railroads were throwing rails west all along the line, first at Saint Joseph, Missouri, where the Hannibal and St. Joseph touched the eastern boundary of the Pony Express, and then as far west as San Francisco. Pop was against railroads; he had the feeling they were an invasion of his privacy, that with the steel rails would come the end of a way of life. Benjie argued with him, pointing out that the market for their steers was coming closer every day. Soon there would be no need to bulldoze a herd of cattle up the Great Western or the Chisholm to Dodge City.

"Trail drives is going out of style, Pop."

"Like gunfighters," Kinniston said suddenly.

They stared at him. His shoulders moved faintly. "The sign's clear to read. Amnesty for outlaws in the Territory, Judge Parker in the Oklahoma country. A new breed of people is coming west on those railroads and along the Oregon Trail. God-fearing folk, bringing family bibles in their wagons. Men like Jim Courtright in Fort Worth and Wyatt Earp in Dodge City are part of the movement. Lawmen, helping to make a good land for the bible readers when they get here."

He broke off abruptly; Fay could see the restlessness come into his face, into the sudden glance of his eyes. He moved from the mantel across the room, skirting Pop's chair, to slide out onto the porch. Fay could see him staring into the distance with his head slightly tilted to one side, as if he were using a sense known only to the wild things of the world. After a moment he came back inside.

"Supper's almost ready," she told him. Then, "Pop, show Mr. Kinniston the map you had that surveyor fellow draw. Give him an idea why Fencepost is fightin' us so hard."

There was a rolltop desk pushed back against the wall with a faded chromo hung above it. Old newspapers—the *Rocky Mountain News* and a frayed copy of the *Tombstone Nugget*—covered its top, sharing space with a thick layer of dust. Pop pushed the straightback chair out of the way and reached into one of the cubbyholes for a roll of heavy paper. As he spread it out across his knee, sitting on the edge of the straightback, Kinniston saw the paper was covered with lines and curves and tight, small printing.

Pop moved a grimey fingernail along a series of wriggling lines. "That's Butterwood Creek, Triangle's southern boundary. Runs out of the Indian Lances over eastward, to Wardance and beyond. Meets the North River somewhere around Bearpaw, I understand. This here wedge of land is Triangle, with the base edging the creek."

It was shaped like a slice of pie, narrowing at the top. On either side of that cone was Fencepost land, forming a great sweep or arc to east and north where it spread out for a fifty-mile run toward Wardance.

"All crackerjack graze, every foot of it," Pop admitted. "Young—Bib Young, who owns Fencepost—wants Triangle. You can see why." The dirty fingernail touched the creek and ran along it. "Near ninety miles of creek my land fronts on. Fencepost's got something less'n fifty.

"I moved in here 'bout October, November of '63. Benjie was only ten then, Fay hadn't been born. She's lived here all her life. It's her home, mister. And Fencepost wants it."

The old man was beaten by his defeats at the hands of the weather, by the hard men in Wardance, by steers that died of the colic and of rifle bullets. The furrows in his wind-beaten; sun-scorched face were deep, giving him a sadness in repose that touched at Kinniston, deep down in some part of him that had been long neglected. A fringe of unkempt, untidy white hair rimmed the old man's head. A man without purpose might have hair like that, untended because nobody cared.

Pop sighed, and stared at the map he had drawn. He said heavily, "Damn Fencepost! Damn Gib Young, too."

Benjie had been walking up and down the little room, touching a chairback with trembling fingertips, licking his lips nervously while staring at a dusty chromo he'd seen a thousand times and more. Kinniston knew anger and frustration were on fire in him. The fire was all but out in his father.

"Couple of years ago he came to Wardance, this Gib Young," Pop said patiently, in his tired voice. "A tall, quiet man with a habit of gambling for big stakes. He won a pot here, a pot there. Nobody knows how much. Shad Tremaine owned Frencepost then. Shad never cared much for Young. They was always at each other's throats with words. One night they played poker together.

"Nobody around Wardance ever seen such cards as Gib Young got. Even when Tremaine did the dealing, Young won. Course, folks knew Young was cheatin' those times he dealt, though nobody caught him at it. It was like Shad was jinxed."

Kinniston smiled tightly, going over the ways a man could cheat even when somebody else was handling the cards. Wardance was a backwater town, far enough off the herd trails to keep the drifters away. The card sharps never bothered with the little towns, where the money was always tight.

"Young won everything Tremaine had—ranch, cattle, horses. Tremaine went to get a cash loan to pay him off. There was a gunshot. When folks ran out into the street they found Tremaine dead in an alleyway, a gun in his hand, his brains blown out."

Pop shrugged. "Young had nothing to do with that, though. He was sitting in front of fifty men in the Murchison when it happened."

Kinniston said gently, "So Gib Young became cattle king on the strength of a few card hands. I've seen it happen in a lot of places."

Benjie flared, "Tell him where Tremaine was shot. Go ahead, tell him. He's a gunman, he'll know what everybody else knows but is too damn scared to talk about."

Pop nodded slowly. "Tremaine shot himself—or is supposed to've shot himself, in the left temple. He used his right hand all the time. His gun was found in his right hand."

"Reads like murder," Kinniston agreed.

"But who? Who? There was no stranger in town that night. Young couldn't have done it. Everybody in Wardance and on the range was Shad's friend."

Fay heard her chickens hissing in the oven, went and opened the door, using a patchwork cut for a holder. The fowls were nicely browned, the potatoes big and puffy where she'd slit their skins. She tried to move as quietly as possible, walking on tiptoe so as to hear the low voices in the next room. Benjie was easy to hear, she thought affectionately. He roared and shouted. Even Pop's worn voice floated through to her. Kinniston spoke softly, almost in a whisper. It was hard to hear him. More than once she was forced to pause before setting a plate and a knife and fork on the table, to listen with her head tilted to one side.

Kinniston was talking now. "—a federal marshal. All you have to do is write a letter to get one down in this section of the Lances."

"A letter!" Benjie snorted. "Before it gets posted we'll be—"

"Benjie!" snapped Pop warningly.

Pop said something else, so quietly the girl couldn't hear him. She bit her lip, fright mushrooming like a hard, quick pain in her midsection. She put her hand to her side, trying to fight down a sudden wash of hysteria.

"—not gunfighters! All I've shot in my life has been a few deer and rabbits. Young has the gunfighters.

The Kid. A man who calls himself French John. And worst of all, the marshal himself. Man named Kesselring, Luther Kesselring."

"I've heard of French John," Kinniston admitted, thinking back.

It had been at a trading post, three years ago, just when he'd taken up the long trail after Red Patsy and the others. There had been a drunken Indian, a Mimbreno—it was Apache country, in among the Mogollons—who was making himself a nuisance. Drunk and with his hides gone, he came wandering back, demanding more of the rotgut whiskey the post sold. He had an empty jar in his hand. Finally one of the men playing poker had come to his feet, turned the 'Pache and booted him out through the batwing doors.

Everybody thought that was the end of it but ten minutes later the redskin was back, staggering blindly this time, holding out the jar. Another few minutes and he would be sleeping it off. The man who'd booted him got up to do it again when a heavyset man with a blackish beard stubble pushed in front of him.

"I'll 'andle thees one," he said with a hard grin.

He yanked the jar from the red fingers, lifted it and brought it crashing down over the greasy black hair. The Mimbreno dropped as if shot. Then the heavyset man picked him up and heaved him out of the room.

Somebody said, "Nice work, French John," and everyone laughed. Kinniston had not laughed; in reality he was paying little attention to what went on around him, nursing his solitary drink, thinking about the three men he burned to kill. The name French John and the stubble-bearded face hung in his memory, and the fact that next morning the 'Pache had been found dead around back of the post, his skull split open.

Fay came to the door between the living room and

kitchen. "Food's on. Pop, you an' Benjie wash up around back." She wanted a minute to talk to the lean man.

When she heard their boots clomp down the porch steps she put a hand on his forearm and looked up at Kinniston. "Is it bad? About Fencepost and us, I mean? I couldn't hear one time when Pop was whispering."

"No," he said slowly. "not bad."

Kinniston felt a touch of shame. I stand here and lie to her with my poker face on, because it is very bad for these people. He had played this game himself and seen it played, many times. Except that the other Pop Mercers had hired gunfighters themselves and sent them up against the big ranchers. It had been Kinniston's job to cut them down, to strip them away from the little landholders so the big ranchers could move in. I wish there was something I could do, but I can't help. I can only ride out of their lives. If I knew any prayers I would pray. After supper he would be gone west toward Wardance. In a sense, he would be running away.

chapter 3

His paralyzed cheek was hurting again. It always hurt Gib Young under the stress of emotion; a doctor had told him once that when a man was angry or frightened the blood moved faster through his veins. The blood was what caused the pain, trying to force a passage through damaged tissues. He put a hand to his cheek and rubbed gently, keeping his eyes on young Cranford.

"Tell me again, Kid. Tell me what you did."

"I already told you three times. How many times you want to hear it?"

"Once more. This time tell me everything."

The Kid let his eyes drop away from the hard glance Young threw at him. Gib Young had eyes something like that stranger's, down by the creek. They looked deep inside him and saw him for what he was. The Kid could bluster most men around Wardance. He couldn't bluster Gib Young. Or Luther Kesselring or French John, for that matter. Or this stranger.

"I rode onto Triangle graze. I saw three steers. I shot 'em." He hesitated, turning his hat over and over in his fingers. "I—ah—saw Fay Mercer swimmin' in the creek."

"And you stared and wouldn't let her come out."

"How'd you know that?"

Young closed his eyes wearily. After a while you kept seeing the same men over and over again, from one town to the next. Men never seemed to change. The Kid was just one more young braggart, a bully when he could get away with it, too dumb to realize his wasn't the only fast gun or anything more than even passing fast. Dutch Korman could let the Kid hold his Colt in his hand and still beat his bullet out of its barrel. So could a few handpicked others. Abel Kinniston for one, if Abel were alive and not dead in some unmarked grave down Starvation Peak way.

"I just know, Kid," he said, moving the hand over his cheek again and again. "I just know."

"Well, I didn't mean no harm. Just funnin' with her. I'd a give her her clothes if he—"

"Ah," said Young with a sigh. "Now we're getting to it. Who was this 'he' you speak of?" He knew it wasn't either of the Mercer men. They weren't the kind to frighten the Kid, and the Kid had been badly frightened. Gib Young knew enough about human nature to read the signs as the Kid rode in. His strut was wider, his voice louder, his cockiness more exasperating than ever. The Kid had been trying to build himself up in his own eyes, glueing up the pieces of his pride and trying to join them back together again.

Now the Kid stood uneasily before the big mahogany desk Gib Young had sent East to Philadelphia for, while Young sat at his ease in the big matching chair. Late afternoon sunlight filtered through the drawn blinds. In an hour a breeze would come up to relieve the heat. The blinds would be lifted then, and the windows opened. Until they were, he would sit here at his desk and be uncomfortable, with sweat soaking his armpits and collar, and act the big rancher.

Something or someone had etched fear in the Kid. Gib Young wanted to hear a name, to search his memory of the past for that name, to learn which of a very few men might be riding unattended and alone into this country he had made his own. A man held a piece of land in subjection when he kept a finger to its pulsebeat, knowing who came and went, which man spoke out against him and for how long, what action a rebellious few might take against his tyranny. Gib Young held Wardance in his grip in such a way, and did not mean to let it go.

The Kid said, "I never saw him before."

"What's he look like?"

"Big man, on the lean side. Not old, not young. Hard face with a heavy tan and flat cheekbones. Cold blue eyes, black hair. He was wearing black, too."

Gib Young started and his hand pressed hard against his cheek. "Wearing black?" he asked in a hollow voice.

The Kid stared. He'd never seen the boss jump like that, as if the Kid had touched a raw nerve. He began to relish this; he had no love for Gib Young, only for the hundred dollars a month and keep he paid for his hired gun.

"Why yeah," he said more slowly, watching the rancher closely. "Black shirt, black pants, black shell-belt, black hat, black boots. It was kind of monotonous."

Gib Young caught the faint hint of mockery in those flat tones. Anger flared in him, but only briefly. He drew in the reins of his control and he smiled. "Scared you, didn't he?"

"Not me he didn't."

"You're a liar, Kid. He looked right down into your mean little soul and knew you for what you are, same as I'm doing right now." He watched the Kid look away, and silent laughter rocked him. "The old breed, Kid. He was one of the old breed. They don't build them like that any more. Most of them have passed on. Only a few are left."

The Kid sneered, "The old breed. You sound like somebody's gran'pa!"

Young looked at him hard and the Kid flushed. Mildly he said, "Maybe, maybe." He had a use for the Kid and anyone he could use Gib Young remained on friendly terms with. "Could be I'm getting old."

The Kid fidgeted. "Hell, I didn't mean that. It's just—well, you talk as if this stranger was as fast as French John."

"A man I knew once was faster. Lots faster."

"You mean Wild Bill."

"Hickok? I wasn't thinking of him. You ever hear of Abel Kinniston?"

The Kid shook his head. "Yes, but Kinniston's dead."

"Like Hickok."

The room was suddenly cold to Gib Young. He shivered inside his alpaca coat. He said dreamily, "Kinniston was a wild one. Oh, not mean or crazy like some. He lived alone on the trails like an animal. Untamed. If you wanted his gun, you passed the word around; one day he'd show up at your ranch or your store. He would do the job, get paid and ride off. You never knew where he came from or where he went."

"He don't sound human."

"Sometimes I used to wonder if he was. I never saw him draw but I knew damn fast men he killed in fair fights with a faster gun." Young sighed and moved his shoulders. "Goddam, maybe I'm getting old, sitting here mooning about a dead man."

The Kid was fascinated, he saw. His mouth was open a little and the light of hero worship glistened in his eyes. Young chuckled. He kept forgetting the Kid was so young. Young men were brave or stupid, whichever word you wanted to pin on them. They threw themselves at barriers a wiser man would walk around.

Young said, "You still practice your draw every day?"

"Maybe every other day," the Kid muttered.

Young smiled. "Satisfied you're about as fast as you can get, are you?"

"I'm fast. Never met nobody faster. Except maybe French John."

"You think French John is fast, do you?"

"You know somebody faster?"

Gib Young fought down his irritation. These young fools always had to learn the hard way. He said quietly, "Go get French John and bring him here."

When the Kid was gone out the door and through the front hall, Young came up from his chair and moved across the thick Brussels carpet to the heavy iron safe that squatted under the deerhead wallmount, close beside the huge sideboard. Gib Young had left the Fencepost ranch house much as it had been before he won it from Shad Tremaine. The big desk and chair, the iron safe, the leather easychair that had also come from Philadelphia: these were his own additions. The rich damask drapes, the Argand lamps, the massive furniture, were Tremaine inheritance. With the blend of old and new, the room had a rich, almost luxurious air to it.

He knelt and moved the safe dial crisply, surely.

When the heavy door eased open he reached into a slot and brought out a contrivance of straps and metal strips, fitted to a small, powerful spring. He was about to close the safe door when his gaze brushed a long narrow metal box. Young bit his lip, frowning. He leaned forward and put his fingers over its lid and tugged. The box moved but the lid did not come up. Still locked. His lips twitched. He swung the door shut and twirled the dial.

Carrying the leather and spring contrivance to his desk, he removed his coat and slipped his right forearm into the straps. He buckled them tightly and shook his arm back and forth. The straps clasped tightly, but not so tightly that they would impede circulation.

From a desk drawer he drew out a small .41 derringer and slid it into the clips protruding from the metal strips. The derringer was caught, held firmly, by the spring set. Gib Young drew a deep breath. His right arm jerked forward. The spring shot the derringer forward into his hand. Instinctively, with the ease of old habit, his hand caught it, his forefinger curling about the trigger.

"Fast," he breathed. "Fast as hell, still."

And yet—

It might not be fast enough. With the sleeve of his shirt he wiped his sweat-wet forehead. The old breed, he had said. Well, he was one of the old breed, too. With this holdout gun he had killed his share of men. He thought of the Kid and smiled. He used to eat young braggarts like the Kid for breakfast. Be a pleasure to teach him a lesson, it surely would. But he had need of the Kid. The Kid would throw himself at any barrier Gib Young pointed out. The stranger who had come riding across Triangle land might be such a barrier. He shrugged into the alpaca coat.

He had not killed in several years, not since that unforgotten afternoon in Starvation Peak country. Sometimes a man grows rusty about such things. He lives off the fat land and he births a conscience. It was a man without a conscience who had stood in a rock cluster three years before and put a bullet into Abel Kinniston.

Funny I should keep thinking about Kinniston, who is dead and buried. He always wore black though, and the Kid gave me a start when he mentioned that stranger. If Kinniston were alive to come riding into Wardance country like a gaunt gray ghost, with his magic draw and his wild animal nature—

Young drew a handkerchief across his face. The paralyzed cheek was hurting again. "I got to stop remembering. I'm jumpy on account of them damn Mercers. Wasn't for them I'd have all the creek bottom, places like Pasternak's, Carey's strip, Magruder's farm. Mercer gives them the backbone to refuse to sell out."

He was tired of playing with Corb Mercer. Only thing to do was ride in some night and rub them out, all of them, even the girl. Fire would do it. Fire would destroy anything, even human bodies. There would be no proof of who'd done the shooting or setting fire to the shack they called a ranch house.

The sound of boots came from the front porch. Gib Young smiled and reached for his humidor, bringing out a cigar. He was touching a match to its tip when the Kid came in with French John. Smoking like this, using a cigar for a prop, would make him seem unconcerned when he told them what it was he wanted. Not that the Kid or French John would ask questions. For the money he paid, they obeyed like dumb beasts. Maybe he was trying to draw a picture of himself in his own mind, the image of the big rancher, the builder of the cattle empire. He needed that picture to look at while he talked. . . .

He waited on the porch until the hoofbeats drummed away to the northeast and the Triangle ranch house. His hand lay flat against the porch rail, moving back and forth slowly, all the while his ears held to the fading sound of the dozen men he'd sent on a death mission. When he took away the hand the palm was red and swollen from the pressure he had been exerting.

Gib Young drew a deep breath, moving his right arm gently, feeling the snugness of the holdout straps. The belt across his middle felt tight. He was putting on weight down there; too much easy living, too many heavy meals. Be better if he got out with the hands, helped at the branding fires or rode a boundary line from time to time. With slow steps he came down off the porch and quartered across the yard toward the barns.

A shadow stirred to life at his coming.

"Saddle me up, Crow."

The Indian did not speak. Young had to strain to hear the soft pad of his moccasined feet. Inside of three minutes Little Crow came out leading a rangy gray. The gray threw its head against the reins, slobbering to grip the bit between its teeth. Its hooves danced lightly, as if on air.

"He's full of pepper," said Gib Young admiringly. "Well, I'll get that out of him before sunup." He swung into the kak with the ease of long practice. "You go to bed, Crow."

He left the Indian staring after him, motionless in the barn-door shadow. Little Crow had come with the ranch, like its furniture. Young had kept him on, for the Indian knew horses—had a way with them, as Gib Young had a way with cards, as Dutch Korman had a way with a gun. Sometimes, though, the Indian looked at him with hard black eyes and uneasiness went crawling down Young's spine on icy feet. Ought to have the Kid put a bullet in the Piute some day. Get rid of him as he'd rid himself of so many others during the years.

The years, where did they go?

Tiptoe, tiptoe, they went, and left no traces other than the deeper lines on a man's face and the heavier weight of his soul on the sleepless nights when all he could do was look up at a blank ceiling and wonder at himself, marveling how far he'd come since those years with Major Randolph Pinkney and the Army of the Confederacy. It was fifteen or so years since that afternoon at Appomattox when Grant came riding in on Cincinnatus, his horse, still wearing his fatigue shirt, and Lee meeting him like the gentleman he was, his iron-gray whiskers cut short.

Twenty-five then, he'd been. Georgia born and without the plantation—damn Will Sherman and his Armies of the Tennessee, of the Cumberland, of the Ohio! He had gone back to The Oaks and was forever after sorry for it. Charred timbers and weeds growing out of the ruins. No more slave shacks, no summer hours overlooking the slow waters of the Cossawatee river. Sherman had swept it all away.

He supposed he'd gone a little crazy, after that. Work was beneath his dignity, but he could play cards and cheat with the best of them, so cleverly nobody could ever prove a thing. Two years on the Mississippi, three years beating west through the cattle towns like Dodge City, Abilene, Ogallala. Took him that long to admit what he had become.

The gray moved at its easy pace through the breaks south of the ranch house, making good time. The moon was almost at its full overhead. There was the lemon smell of sage in the night air. Once it had been the same moon and the scent of magnolia, but that was long ago, in another world.

"I *am* getting old," he said.

The gray snorted and he eased his pull on the rein, letting it run. Old? He was not yet forty. Ought to get himself a wife, maybe. Not in town, though; none of those saloon floosies for him. Yet he knew no other women. The settlers' girls smiled at him but for the most part they were a sorry lot. That blond one, that Fay Mercer, was pretty enough, but she hated his guts. Probably be better if he went on the way he was, seeing Ginny every so often in the upper room of the Prairie Queen, forget his dreams of building a cattle kingdom for his sons to inherit.

The moraines were to the west, low and black against a setting sun. Town was not far away now. His boot toe brushed the gray, sent it into a headlong gallop. He rode straight up in the cavalry seat, reins in his left hand always, keeping the right free for his saber. His lips twisted mockingly as he looked down inside himself. He had broken his cavalry saber in a fit of proud rage, minutes after Lee scrawled his big signature on the surrender papers. The saber rusted now, wherever the pieces might be.

Wardance always broke into view with an abruptness that made him want to rub his eyes. The gray came up the long ridge slope as usual and when it reached the crown, why, the town lay there before him, blazing with kerosene lamps and noise. Gib Young liked a town run free and easy. The good citizens of Wardance, and these were no more than a handful, lived on the north side of town in dark houses closed against the light and sound. Young often wondered what time they went to bed. In all the years of his living here, he could not recall ever having seen a lamp on in any of those houses.

He put the gray to a sidling trot moving onto Main Street, smiling a little at the tinny piano in the Glory Hand. Be a mercy to throw out that pile of junk and buy Fats Peters a new one. His gaze went on, touching the Prairie Queen, the Murchison, the Striped Deck, the Desert Rose. They were all the same, with their high false fronts and porch overhangs, long bars and hooded lamps. The barkeeps were fat, heavyset men in shirt sleeves with fancy armbands and aprons. The women were loud, garish, too noisy. Only Ginny was a little different, slim and dark, with a hint in her proud black eyes of what she had been in the past.

The reflections of their batwing doors and lighted windows lay along the hardpacked dirt of Main Street, touching Young and the gray as they moved slowly at a walk through the alternate layers of light and darkness. The miners out of the river diggings were stomping out a reel in the Desert Rose. Young could see the dust rising from under their boots and thought that most men were like little children, easy to please, easy to dominate, easy to rob. All it took was a firm hand and a ready wit.

From the middle of town he could see the marshal's house as a small rectangle of roof shingles and gingerbread woodwork set back from the town well and fenced around by white picketing. A single lamp burned in the front parlor. From time to time a shadow moved in the room. Dutch Korman must—no, not Dutch Korman any more, but Luther Kesselring; he and Dutch had decided that a long time ago—Luther Kesselring must be entertaining his redhead. Luther would never show himself so plainly through a window.

Young swung down at the tierail, looped the reins. Suddenly he felt tired, listless. His glance raked the town once, swiftly and savagely, before he pushed open the picket gate and moved up the path between the hydrangea bushes. Took a lot out of a man to run a stolen ranch, a stolen town. He wondered sometimes if it was worth the trouble.

His knuckles beat against the front-door panelling.

A voice said something in the house; there was a giggle, and a slap of hand on bared flesh. Bootheels thudded on worn flooring.

"Who's there?"

"Gib Young, Luther, Open up."

The door swung back. Young saw the star badge first, winking in the lamplight from the front parlor, then the cowhide vest, the flat-planed face and pale yellow hair of the big German. A heavy shellbelt angled across his hips, weighted by a Colt Peacemaker. Even in his pleasures he needed the gun. There was something symbolic about it, Young thought, but he was too tired to pursue the idea.

"Why Mr. Young, come in." Kesselring chuckled.

"You got Bertha here?" he asked, stepping over the sill.

"She's in the bedroom, which is the best place for her." His hand pushed the door shut. "Anything wrong?"

"Maybe, maybe not. Get rid of her for a little while."

"Look, Gib—"

"Oh, hell. It's only for a little while. Something's come up. A stranger rode onto Triangle land today. He spooked the Kid just by looking at him."

The German considered that, head tilted to one side, and his eyes narrowed. After a moment he grunted and went into the bedroom. Young moved up and down the front parlor, restless, uneasy. He could hear Bertha protesting, and in a way he didn't blame the girl. Damn nuisance to get dressed and go out into the night air when she was liquored up so nicely and probably down to her corset cover. But the stakes in this game were too big to be sentimental. Let a saloon girl hear something and, by God, it was all over town by morning. Gib Young didn't want that.

Kesselring came to the bedroom door and closed it, put his back to the panelling and staring at him. "She's gone out the back way."

"Hate to do this, Dutch. Hate like hell to do it." He told Dutch about the Kid being scared. "Not just anybody can scare the Kid, Dutch. He's too young and stupid to spook easy. Not the Mercers, not anyone we know in Wardance country."

"A stranger, the Kid said," murmured the marshal, moving with his easy stride across the room to sink into a Morris chair.

Gib Young watched him, knowing a momentary pleasure that the big German was taking this as seriously as he had. For a while, a little earlier, he'd wondered about himself going off on a hairtrigger this way over nothing at all, with only a vague feeling of trouble coming, like an intuition.

Kesselring looked up. "Want me to ride out there, come sunup?"

"Yes, but not for the reason you think. I sent French John and the Kid to Triangle with ten riders. I told 'em to kill everybody they found at the Mercer place, then burn it down."

"Little highhanded, isn't it?"

"A fire'll burn out everything. Dead bodies, deeds, clues of any sort. I'll pay for their funerals, naturally. What I want you to do is ride over there and give everything a look. If anybody asks you, say Mercer complained about three of his cows being shot. Make sure the boys didn't leave anything behind to tie in what happened with me."

"In my official capacity as town marshal."

"Exactly."

"I'll be there a little after sunrise if Bertha doesn't tire me out too much."

"See she doesn't, Dutch. Stakes we're playing for are too high to let slip for a floosie."

Kesselring looked pained. "I like Bertha, goddamit. I like her a lot. She's fun to be with."

Young laughed and spread his hand. "My apologies. I forgot I used to be a gentleman, once upon a time." He picked up his beige Stetson. "Who do you think he is, Dutch? The stranger, I mean."

The German smiled lazily. "Got you worried, hasn't he?"

"Frankly, yes. I know the Kid. He must have seen hellfire waiting for him in the stranger's eyes."

"Not many men can get down into a person like that, just with his eyes." Kesselring pushed a hand along his thigh as if to rub sweat off the palm. "Only ones I ever knew could do it were Earp, Hickok, maybe Hardin. Oh yes, and Abel Kinniston."

Young was through the doorway onto the porch, but he turned back to stare. "Funny you should mention him. I've been thinking about Kinniston all night, ever since I talked with the Kid."

"Forget him, he's dead."

"Yes," said Young heavily, "he's dead. So is Hickok, so is Hardin. Who the hell *was* that stranger?"

"You think Mercer hired himself a gun?"

"How could he pay him?"

Dutch Kesselring grunted, staring at the floor. He had risen from the chair, stood solid and phlegmatic, clothes a little rumpled, grease spots on shirt and vest.

Looking at him, you'd never pick him out as a fast gun, but there were almightly few any faster. Maybe nobody, maybe nobody at all. Dutch Korman was still alive in Marshal Luther Kesselring, his gun oiled and ready.

"Dutch," he said suddenly, "you still practice your draw?"

"Huh? Oh, sure. Every day."

Young smiled affectionately. "The Kid doesn't. Every other day's enough."

Dutch snorted contemptuously, then laughed. "Damn little fool."

Gib Young went out into the night and down the porch steps with a warm feeling in his chest. It was good to have a man like Korman siding you. His own gunhand was greased lightning with that holdout, but he was no professional the way Dutch was. The two of them made an unbeatable combination. As he went up into the leather and settled his rump he thought about Ginny. Some of his earlier worry was gone, now he'd seen the German. Might be he'd step in and say hello, since he was in town.

He told himself he was a fool to bother his head about the stranger. What could one man do against Dutch Korman and French John and the Kid? The weight of the holdout gun strapped to his right forearm reminded him that he had never forgotten how to use it. Be a good idea to do some practicing himself.

chapter 4

Abel Kinniston made distance at a steady run, with the Nez Perce striding smoothly under his weight. The rolling grazelands were far below him this high in pine timber, but their gentle lift and fall hung in his heart with the memory of an elfin face and slant eyes and the long ripple of blonde hair. He could not shake the feeling that he was running away.

He pulled in the palouse, turning to rest a palm on its croup, sending his eyes back along the trail. A frown lay across his face. No place, no woman, ever had held him for very long. No reason at all why he should keep remembering Fay Mercer and her ranch, her Paw and brother. Twice now he had stopped and looked back through the screening branches of the tall pines, pas the humped rocks and flat reaches of the Indian Lances. His eyes lifted to the moon with part of its edge chipped away. He was restless, unsure of himself, this night, which came of touching elbows with a girl at a dinner table. It showed a man what he missed by living as a wolf lives, in the wild places.

"Made my choice a long time ago," he said softly, and lifted the reins.

He let the horse walk on over the needled floor and up higher where the wind came cold and raw through the firs and spruces. Kinniston shivered in the light flannel shirt, glad for the mackinaw wrapped in his bedroll. Up this high it was still winter. Further on there were patches of snow to be seen, gleaming like silver under the moon. The mountain waters gushing in their beds would be liquid ice, so cold it would hurt the teeth to drink.

When his shivering became a steady thing he halted the appaloosa and turned to loosen the buckles of his bedroll. His gaze lifted to the flatlands stretched below and to the gleam of moonlight on—

No, it was not moonlight, for the moon was something made of burnished silver and this was a hot red color blazing down there, far below.

Red was the color of blood, of fire.

"Fire? Somebody's hayrick going up, probably."

He looked more closely, taking his time. After a moment he shivered again, but it was not the cold that sent that quiver down his spine. He had made a mistake, was all. When he had turned, those other times on the trail, he could not see the Triangle ranch house; it seemed he could, but he had been mistaken. Now he could see the place where he'd eaten dinner this night, and it was a solid blotch of red flame eating upward into the night sky.

"Oh Christ," he said softly, and his fingers fell from the bedroll buckles. A hand swung the palouse. His toe jammed its ribs.

He fled downtrail like a shadow slipping silently and swiftly between the pine boles, skirting the clumps of quaking aspen rustling in the wind. The palouse caught his excitement, folding itself into the running, seeming to sense the rocks it must avoid, the narrow braid of path down which its hooves must fly. They fell together out of the high mountain slopings into the plateau lands, and then horse and rider merged with the ponderosa pines to come at last into the pinons and the sagebrush. Down here the ground leveled off, made the running easier.

He came straight across Checkerboard land and onto Triangle, the same way he'd gone out, but now he came with his flannel shirt wind-stuck to his chest, with the black Stetson pulled low above his eyes, the brim flapping. His heart was frightened in his ribcase, remembering the way the Mercers had talked this afternoon and at the dinner table later, recalling the hopelessness and the stubbornness in their faces. The hopelessness would be there still, only worse; the stubbornness would be gone. There was nothing left to fight for, with the ranch house gone like this.

The fire grew and grew in his sight and then lay across the sky red and vivid, with the smoke a stink in his nostrils as the palouse pounded closer and closer. His eyes hunted the redness, seeking Fay or one of the others. There was no one to be seen, only the fire roaring uncontrolled.

Kinniston was leaping from the leather before the horse could slide to a halt, hitting on a foot and stumbling forward, pulling at the black kerchief at his throat, yanking it up to cover the lower part of his face.

The heat was awful. Nobody could live inside that holocaust. Either the Mercers had made it out to safety or—

"Fay," he shouted. "Fay, do you hear me?"

The flames roared louder, higher, beating at his eardrums with the muffled thunder of their growth. He ran around the ranch house, hunting desperately with his eyes, sick in his middle, watching to retch.

"Fay! Fay Mercer!"

He thought he heard a wail come drifting from the

red flames. He ran for the searing heat, seeing the old ranch house like a black outline encased all in vivid pale crimson. The fire roared at him like an animal, its tongues beating in the wind. He put his feet toward what had been the back porch and came as close as he dared.

"Pop? Benjie?" he bellowed.

Again he thought he heard that voice, summoning him as the Lorelei are said to summon travelers along the Danube. It was a quick, harsh cry, filled with despair. And with death? If he could get anyone out, he would gladly risk the flames.

"Fay? Fay?"

He ran in against the porch with an arm upflung against the awful heat. It burned his face; he felt, as he stood there, that he was getting cooked. He was, too. He could smell scorched flesh. It made him want to gag.

"Hell, nobody can go in there."

He turned, and then he heard the crack of wood, the rush of blazing timbers. He whirled, crying out, seeing the porch columns and their roof breaking free and buckling, falling, coming down at him. His right arm came up and warded them off, giving a little to their weight, but the fire was leaping to his shirt and the pain was frightful. He cursed as he ran from the collapsing roof, bent against the agony, snapping buttons as he hurled the blazing shirt from him.

He panted, sliding to a stop and staring down at his right arm. There was no hair on it, and it stank. In a little while it would begin to hurt like hell because the skin was burned. Not badly, but badly enough. It would lay him up a couple of weeks, a burn like that. In a few hours he wouldn't be able to move the arm without pain.

He must get to a mountain stream where there would be river mud, and plaster his arm with that rich black goo which soothed the flesh and aided its healing, just as the Indians used it against the bite of burned flesh. And he had no time to waste. Everyone was dead here at Triangle. Abel Kinniston ran for the spotted stallion.

Then he heard the sobbing in the high grasses and he angled his run from the horse to the blue grama. It was Fay Mercer, lying there, moaning. It must have been her voice he heard before, when he believed it came from inside the house.

He bent over her, seeing her skirt burned away until most of her legs were revealed, white and slim against the grass. A smoldering blanket lay nearby. She must have snatched it up and come running as the flames swirled all around.

His hand touched her shoulder and she turned, clutching a gun beneath her, lifting it toward him. Kinniston slammed the edge of his left hand—it hurt to move his right—against her wrist even as he lurched sideways. The gun belched flame at him. He felt the bullet nudge his armpit, heard it go whining upward into darkness.

She lay on her back, eyes wide.

"I thought you—one of them—"

"Them?"

"Fencepost riders. French John. Bobby Cranford. Others with them. They shot Pop and Benjie, me too...."

For the first time he saw that there was blood on her shirtwaist. Gently he opened the blouse, probing her shoulder, seeing the blood well out onto her skin. "Bullet's out, which is a blessing. Must've gone right through you."

"I'm going to kill them all," she whispered. "All of them. One by one I'll make them pay." She shuddered, and tears welled from her wide eyes. It was a silent crying she was doing, as if her grief were so bitter and deep inside her that it came out almost silently.

Her eyes widened at sight of his naked chest. "Your shirt. What happened?"

"Burned my arm, back there at the porch."

She was all soft sympathy, ignoring her own hurt to lift his hand and study his scorched flesh. Her eyes told him she knew he was in pain. "I'd put butter on it if I had any. Next best thing is wet mud."

He grinned, showing his teeth, "I know." He hesitated, then asked, "Where's the nearest doctor?"

She shook her head, making her blond hair dance. "No doc nearer than Wardance, and I won't go in there. The Kid will finish us both off then, with the whole damn town cheering him on."

Her voice was bitter. Kinniston could understand her feelings. He grunted. "Next best thing is to ride for the hills. Might find us some chokeberry bushes there. The Cheyenne treat their wounds with crushed chokeberry roots."

"No sense us standing here just talking," she agreed.

He put his left arm around her middle to help her walk. She was small but there was a solid, womanly feel to her slim body. Like whipcord, she was, soft and pliable but strong beneath the softness. A strand of her thick yellow hair blew across his face and he could smell her fragrance. The wound in her shoulder was not serious. There were a couple of clean shirts in his warbag. He could put a bandage around her upper arm and left shoulder as well as anyone, even with his left hand.

He asked softly, "They think you're dead, is that it?"

"Yes. Let them think so, until I come back. Otherwise they may make another try for me."

"Pop? Benjie?" he asked gently.

"Shot down like mad dogs soon as they went out on the porch to see what men were riding into the yard big as life, yelling and shouting out insults. Pop got one shot off before he folded over with a .45 slug in his middle. Benjie didn't get a chance to shoot. Five, six bullets hit his chest all at once."

She was speaking hoarsely, with raw hate on her tongue. Kinniston eased her into the kak, waited for her to talk herself out.

"You? What about you?" he whispered.

"Me? Oh, I ran for it, through the kitchen to the back door. Somebody snapped a shot at me. It hit my shoulder. I spun around and fell back inside the kitchen. They must have seen me go down and not move. They thought I was dead too."

She put a hand over her face, bowing forward, trying not to remember the pain and the slow, awful sound of dead bodies being dragged across bare flooring into the big living room, hearing the hoarse laughter of the voices as the boots came to stand around her in a semicircle. A torch flared redly and then another, and then half a dozen of them were being tossed at the house, thudding into red fire as they landed.

"I got to my hands and knees and crawled around, wondering where I could hide. They were outside, laughing like it was the funniest joke in all the world. The fire was just starting but the heat was—so bad...."

Fay shook her head until the blond hair swirled. "I think I went a litle crazy for a while. I remember my skirt being on fire and throwing a bucket of water on it. The pain in my shoulder was pretty bad, too. I didn't dare go outside. They were still there, waiting. Like vultures. They could have shot me again if they'd seen me. After a little while I didn't care whether they saw me or not. I couldn't stay in there. I grabbed a blanket and crawled out. They were gone by that time...."

Kinniston eased a boot into the stirrup, lifting upward. He settled himself behind the cantle and, reaching past her, took the reins in his left hand. The saddler began to walk away from the fire, away from Triangle toward the Indian Lances.

"Where are you taking me?" she asked.

"Into the mountains where you'll be safe."

Her hand touched the tattered skirt which showed the white thigh. "Like this? I'll freeze to death."

"I've an extra pair of pants in my warbag. You can wear them and one of my shirts until we hit Carbine."

"What's Carbine?"

"Outlaw town back in the hills."

They rode in silence after that and as the appaloosa put the miles under its hooves the girl leaned into him more and more heavily, until Kinniston knew she was asleep. He glanced at her tearstained cheeks, at the soft red mouth relaxed in slumber. Her long blond hair blew fitfully in the breeze, touching his mouth, his throat, carrying a subtle perfume in its strands. Much to his astonishment he rather relished the softness of her body against his own. It had been a long time since he'd held a woman in his arms.

Kinniston let the palouse walk until ponderosa pines towered all around them as if trying to touch the stars with their feathery tips, and dawn was a redness in the eastern sky. Not until he heard the sound of water running over bottom stones did he rein in the spotted horse and, gripping the girl by his left hand, aided her slide to the ground.

She looked up at him, face white and pinched, and he understood that her left shoulder was throbbing raw with pain, even as his right forearm was pulsing. Her eyes seemed enormous and her usually good spirits were subdued. Her lips quivered from time to time. Kinniston understood she was fighting tears.

"Chokeberry bushes," he said.

Her face was blank, and he grinned. Teasingly he chuckled. "Easy to see you've never lived with Indians. Here, come along and I'll show them to you."

She helped him pull up the chokeberry stalks, she with her right hand, he with his left. Then, sitting beside him, gravely chewing the roots to a thick paste after washing them in the mountain streams, she felt a quiet companionship such as she had never before known. Her eyes touched the man, sensing the untamed wildness in him, a wildness which was momentarily subdued while he tended their wounds.

The paste was moist, soothing, on her wound, front and back. With a torn shirt, clean but frayed, he made a bandage of sorts which she had to help him tie, for he had no use of his right hand. Then the girl knelt beside the mountain stream and caught up handfuls of muddy ooze, plopping them on the forearm and elbow he held up to her.

"Any better?" she asked.

His arm was quivering with pain, but he smiled. He was a wounded timber wolf, silently enduring its agony. A tightness had come to his lips and a blankness to his eyes that was not caused by his burns; it was a withdrawal of himself against her presence, she understood.

"It'll do," he growled. "It'll take time. I don't expect miracles."

She smiled faintly, glad that he was gruff, knowing that his very gruffness was good for her. If he had been sympathetic she would have been bawling on his shoulder.

She watched him come to his feet and move to the Nez Perce horse. With only his left hand, he unstrapped the saddle, yanked it to the ground, jerked off the saddle blanket. He fastened his lariat to the stallion, making a rope bridle so it could roam between the trees.

He lifted the saddle blanket and came to her where she knelt beside the mountain stream. "You can take my mackinaw; I'll wrap myself up in the blanket."

"Will you be warm enough?"

He let his lips twitch into a smile, looking down at her. There was a concern for his comfort in her face; Abel Kinniston told himself not to be a fool, she would be solicitous to any man in a like situation. Yet it was good to know that it mattered to one person, at least, whether or not he might suffer.

"Come on," he told her, "let's find a tree bole."

When she had the mackinaw on and had spread the horse blanket over them, he eased his spine against the rough bark of a big pine. Her head lay on his chest, his left arm holding her easily. Within moments, Fay was asleep.

The man stared into the blackness of the night. He was violating his first rule of life: never get involved with people. Hell! He could not have let her bleed to death outside her burning home. He was no animal, he was a man, and manhood had its own obligations.

He tried to flex the fingers of his right hand, his gunhand, and could not. Sourly, he wondered what he would do if Dutch Korman or Tom Yancey were to ride up into these hills, come sunup.

A cool breeze sifting through the branches of the juniper bushes and the ponderosa pines brushed against Kinniston. His eyes snapped open and he became aware of a weight lying across his chest. There was a faint fragrance in his nostrils.

He realized then that Fay Mercer was sleeping half on him, and that his arm was about her as though shielding her from the rest of the world. He sought to shift his body, and she murmured unintelligibly.

Kinniston scowled. He didn't like to be saddled with this girl. Always he had been alone. Never before had he been forced to think of or even consider the safety and comfort of another person.

He was too old a dog to learn new tricks.

Gently he maneuvered his body until he was out from under hers. She lay sleeping, and a vagrant breeze tossed the yellow locks of her hair across her face. It was a pretty face, he conceded, but pretty faces meant nothing to Abel Kinniston.

When he was on his feet he grew aware of the pain in his right arm. The pain was not as great as it had been, but it was there, throbbing. He flexed his fingers. Eventually, he supposed, he would have the full use of that arm, but not for a time. Maybe not for a long time.

Kinniston walked to the mountain stream, knelt down. He began to apply the wet mud to his forearm. The coolness felt good; it seemed that the wet mud was slowly drawing out the pain.

He thought as he knelt there, with the mud oozing wet on his arm. If he were alone, he would lose himself in the high trails of the Indian Lances and hide himself much as a wounded wolf might do, until his hurt was better. He could scarcely do that with the girl. She was not used to living like a wild animal; she would probably sicken on him and make things worse.

Kinniston scowled. All this trouble came of getting involved with folks. Still, there wasn't much he could have done about it other than what he had done. He could scarcely have left the girl to die in that fire.

He put more of the wet mud on his arm and sat

there patiently, letting the pain seep out of him. Again and again he flexed his fingers, discovering that he could move them more easily than he had last night. At least his hand hadn't been damaged.

Hunger began to eat in him as his eyes went over the running brookwaters and the stand of box elders beyond it. He had no food, but there was food on the mountain. He had seen jackrabbit tracks and the marks of a deer.

He would go hunt some food for breakfast. At least that would keep him from thinking about the girl and what he was going to do with her. He rose to his feet and moved toward the big pine against which his rifle leaned.

Fay was still sleeping, wrapped in his mackinaw. He paused to study her. She was a pretty thing, all right. Pert, too. And her mouth was shaped for laughter. Too bad about her folks. Their dying in that fire made her homeless.

His left hand swept up the Winchester. Better be on his way. If food was out there to be found, ne meant to find it. This would not be the first time he had hunted for his breakfast, and it would not be his last.

As he walked, he told himself that he was going even higher into these mountains, up there where the Alpine fir trees grew, and the trembling aspen. No one would be able to find him, not when he put his mind to hiding his trail. Besides, there was no reason to expect anybody to be looking for him, or even for the girl. Everyone would assume she had died in that fire.

He went a little more than a mile before he sighted the deer. He froze and raised his rifle very slowly. The deer was munching, its head lowered. Fortunately the wind was blowing toward him; the animal would not suspect his presence.

His finger tightened slowly on the trigger.

The deer sprang aside, went two steps and then crumpled. It was dead when Kinniston came up to it, bent and lifted its body up onto a shoulder. Like that, he began his walk back to Fay and the big pine.

Fay was standing staring at him as he came walking. Her eyes were big frightened pools of blue. When she recognized him some of the tenseness went out of her. She ran toward him, the mackinaw flapping.

"I got scared," she called, sliding to a halt. "I—I thought you'd left me."

"Wouldn't do that."

Her eyes touched the dead dear. "Can I help? What do I do? Will you show me?"

"Be easier if I do it."

Her face lost some of its gaiety, became quiet. "I'm in your way. You don't like having me around, do you.?"

"You're here. I aim to feed you."

"And after that?"

He would not look at her but dropped the deer and went to his knees, reaching for his knife. He began to skin the animal, to cut off sections of meat. Some of the meat he would cook for their breakfast, the rest he meant to preserve by smoking and carry it with them.

Fay was always at his elbow, almost dancing in her eagerness to help. She watched everything he did, how he did it. When he carried off some of the meat to hang on sticks above the fire he had built, she knelt down and began to cut the meat into long, thin strips, just as he had done. He came back and stood over her, watching.

Fay glanced up at him, a challenge in her face. "Well? Am I doing it right?"

"Just fine," he said.

The corners of her mouth quivered into a smile.

She bent her head and went on working, knowing a sudden delight inside her that he had praised her.

They sat side by side under the pine, chewing silently. A big coffeepot that Kinniston carried in a sack was bubbling merrily. When it was ready, he poured a tin cup full of the brew and handed it to the girl.

"Only got one cup," he told her.

"We'll share it," she announced, and took a long sip.

When she handed the cup to him, he hesitated, then put the metal rim to his lips. The coffee was hot and strong and it put a warmth in his body.

"We got to go to Carbine," he said slowly, refilling the cup.

"What's that?"

"A little town up here in the Lances."

Fay stared. "I never heard of any such place."

"You wouldn't be likely to. Not many folks know about it. Just longriders and such, and lonely men."

"An outlaw town?" she asked. "I've heard of them."

"Need supplies. And another cup."

Fay smiled. "Does it bother you so much, drinking from the same one I use?"

"Never had much to do with a female companion. Or even a male. Been alone most of the past few years. Most of my life, come to that."

"You don't like people, do you?"

"Seen too much of what they're like."

Fay stared at the fire where the meat was smoking, remembering Pop and Benjie. They were dead now. She would never see them again. Her lips quivered and tears came into her eyes.

What sort of life had they had, working like dogs, or what? Barely enough to eat, and even that they had to depend on their own ranch to supply, half the time. The storekeepers in Wardance would rarely sell them the goods they needed—on orders from Gib Young, most probably.

Well, she was finished with Wardance. And with that ranch that was now hers. What could one girl do with running a ranch all by herself?

She glanced at Kinniston out of the corners of her eyes. He was sitting, chewing, staring off across the brook. At what? What visions was he seeing, right now? If only he would take her back to Triangle, stay with her and try to make a go of it! Ah, then she would not need to worry any more.

Fay swallowed hard.

In a tiny voice, she asked, "What are you going to do with me?"

Kinniston turned his head slowly, his eyes studying her. "Take you up into the high hills for a spell. Can't very well take you back to Triangle, now can I?"

"No, I suppose not. They'd kill me same as they did Pop and Benjie."

Kinniston scowled. "What kind of men make war on a girl?"

Fay turned more fully to face him and anger tinted her cheeks a dull red. "Gib Young, that's who. He owns Fencepost and he wants the whole valley. He's got gunfighters to back him up. Oh, I don't mean Bobby Cranston. Well, he's one of them, I guess. But there are others. French John, for one."

He nodded, frowning. He knew about French John, all right. He asked, "What about the town marshal? Or is he taking Young's pay?"

Fay shrugged. "They're close, is all I know. What Young wants done, Luther Kesselring does."

"Quite a setup. What about the other ranchers?"

"What can they do? They've seen Tremaine shot down—though they made an attempt to make folks think it was suicide—and now Pop and Benjie are gone." Her chin firmed. "Won't be long before the other ranchers get crowded out too, and then Gib Young will own just about all there is around here."

She got to her feet and walked away.

Kinniston looked after her, knowing she was weeping silent tears for her dead. He wanted to console her, to speak some words that might take away the sting of those deaths, but he was not a man for that type of speech. He felt uncomfortable, ill at ease.

He rose and moved toward the Nez Perce horse, lifting the big saddle and throwing it across its back. He took his time with the cinches and the bridle, and when he was finished, Fay was walking toward him.

Her eyes were red but there were no more tears.

"Get up in the saddle," he said. "I'll break camp and then we'll be on our way."

"I'll help," she said. "It will give me something to do."

She turned away and began to gather up the strips of smoked meat, putting them in the oilskin sack he handed her. She watched him as he moved about, graceful as a wild animal, making certain that the fire was out.

Then she went toward the horse and put a foot in the stirrup. She wondered, as she swung into the kak, how long Abel Kinniston was going to keep her with him.

Fay Mercer shivered. She had no one else to turn to.

chapter 5

Carbine was a tiny place, nothing more than a saloon, a blacksmith shop, and a store. There was a long hitching post in front of the saloon, and out behind the blacksmith shop a fenced corral held a sleepy pony.

It was a lonely place, surrounded on all sides by the spruce and lodgepole pines, and the mountain wind would whistle when it roamed this flat stretch of ground where the sunbaked buildings seemed almost to lean against it. There was no life to be seen, not even a dog. The wind whipped up little whirlpools of dirt and sent them spinning.

Kinniston halted at the break in the trees. His eyes went over the town and found it unchanged since his last visit, some years before. The buildings were as rickety, as baked, as ramshackled as ever. He grunted and glanced up at the girl.

She was staring at the town with wide eyes. Compared to this place, Wardance was a thriving metropolis. She saw Kinniston looking up at her, and grimaced.

"Isn't much, is it?" she asked.

"No need for it to be, as long as it carries whiskey and bullets, and some food. Outlaws use it, for the most part—or did. I've met a few of them in the past."

He moved forward and the Nez Perce horse walked slightly behind him, with Fay Mercer swaying easily in the saddle. They came down the middle of the bare dirt which might be called a street, and when he came to the hitchrail, Kinniston tied the reins.

Fay swung down and looked at him.

Kinniston nodded toward the store. "A few things we'll need to buy."

The store was empty save for an older man who sat dozing behind a counter. At the sound of Kinniston's boots, he snorted, shook himself, and ventured a smile.

"I want grub," Kinniston said. "Plenty of bacon and flour, and some boxes of shells, as many as you got."

He glanced at Fay. "And a coat, if you got one, that will fit the lady."

His purchases were soon ready. Fay lifted off his mackinaw and slipped into the coat he handed her. Then Kinniston caught up the bags in which his purchases had been put, and moved out into the street.

"I want another horse," he said softly. "You wait here."

He moved toward the saloon. As he stepped into it, he moved swiftly to one side until his eyes could become accustomed to the comparative darkness. He saw that the saloon was empty except for the barkeep who had also been dozing. Off to one side of the room a staircase was set against the wall. Kinniston eyed it, then turned to the bartender.

"You rent rooms?" he asked.

The man grinned at him. "Course I do. Got plenty of them at the moment. Nobody else but me lives here right now."

Kinniston nodded, then said, "I need a bronc."

The barkeep frowned. "No horses around, mister. 'Cept for those we own. I mean the men who live here all the year round."

Kinniston smiled coldly. "I'll pay two hundred."

The bartender rubbed his unshaven jaw. Two hundred dollars was a small fortune in Carbine. He sighed, glancing down at his belly. He had put on weight since he had come to this Godforsaken spot. He didn't ride as much as he used to, being content to sit day after day behind his bar.

"Got a pony myself," he admitted. "Tame as a pet. Might not do for you."

"Show me."

The heavyset man led the way out the rear door and walked toward the corral. Kinniston saw the sleepy pony he had noted before. The pony pricked up its ears at the sound of the footfalls and turned its head toward them.

"There he is. Not much to look at, maybe, but he can go all day. He's yours for that two hundred."

"Saddle and bridle go with it?"

The bartender chuckled. "Might as well throw it in. Won't do me any good without the horse to put it on."

Kinniston handed over the money, moved into the corral and brought out the horse. The bartender came out with saddle and bridle and in a few moments the horse was ready to ride.

He led the pony out before the saloon, saw Fay standing and watching. "You got your own mount now."

He tied the sacks filled with food back of the pony and then watched as Fay stepped into the kak. He nodded when he saw the pony shift slightly under her and behave itself.

Mounting himself, he led the way out of town and

toward the higher reaches of the Indian Lances. Up there toward the peaks he would stop and stay for a week or two. By that time his arm ought to be a little better. Besides, it would give him a chance to use his left arm in the handling of a gun.

Years before he had carried two guns, but as time passed he had discarded his left-hand gun, being content with only one. But with his right arm hurt, it might be a good idea to see how fast he still was with his left.

They went for miles between the Douglas firs. In time they came to a little stream of crystal-clear water flowing over white bottom stones, and Kinniston swung the Nez Perce to follow the stream's meandering way upward. The air was cooler here and the wind seemed more vigorous. Glancing back, he saw that Fay was almost hidden in the fleece-lined coat he had bought her.

"We'll camp soon," he said. "Then you can move about and get your blood flowing. Warm you up."

"I'm all right."

"Sure you are. But you'll feel better, just the same."

As the sun was setting they came out into a clearing. Kinniston reined up and sat the saddle, eying it. The little stream was off to one side, gurgling happily, and there was plenty of high grass for the horses. There—in under a big Engelmann spruce—was the perfect spot for their beds.

He came down onto the ground and nodded at her. "This is where we make our camp."

In an hour he had cut a number of branches and made a little lean-to under the big spruce. Fay would sleep there, with a blanket over her. He would make out well enough in his mackinaw, sleeping beside the fire.

They ate the jerked meat and the biscuits which Fay

had made, sharing the same tin cup filled with coffee. Kinniston smiled when he sipped, saying, "Meant to get you a cup of your own, back there in Carbine, but it slipped my mind."

"I don't mind," she murmured.

They sat before the fire until the sunlight disappeared and the stars glittered overhead in a velvety black sky. Fay had seated herself close to him, and for the most part she rested against his big shoulder.

At first he had felt uncomfortable with her shoulder touching his, but as the minutes slipped into hours, he found he was enjoying that contact. Never before had any human being been so dependent on him. If he could have found a safe place to leave this girl, he would have done so, but he knew that to abandon her would be cruel and heartless, almost like condemning her to death.

"Time to sleep," he muttered at last.

Fay stirred. "I was almost asleep," she murmured drowsily. "It was good to be beside you, Abel."

He glanced at her sharply. It had been a long time since anyone had used his first name. A little flush of pleasure ran through him. He snorted. Was he getting soft? Always he had depended on himself alone. There had never been anyone to consider when he made his decisions.

She moved toward the blanket he had spread on the thick grasses. She seemed smaller and more helpless in his eyes as he watched her. What was he going to do with her? He could not abandon her, nor could he take her on the blood trail he followed after Tom Yancey and Dutch Korman.

He would think of something. He always had been able to work out his problems. All he needed was time, and perhaps a little sleep. He rose to his feet and moved away from the fire, staring up at the sky and its stars, letting his gaze rove out across the grasses and the trees.

They were safe enough here, high in the Indian Lances. No one would come looking for Fay Mercer. And no one knew about him.

When he came back he saw that the girl was rolled up in the blanket, and was sleeping. Kinniston drew his mackinaw tighter about him and lay down near the fire. In moments he wa asleep too.

In the first dawn hours he woke and rose, stretching. The fire had died down to a few glowing coals, so he blew on it, added chips, watched it flare up. To it he added sticks and when it was flaring, he tossed a couple of broken branches on the flames.

He began to make coffee, to fry bacon and make biscuits.

Today he would exercise his right forearm, for without its use he would be severely handicapped. Kinniston scowled and glanced at his warbag. In it was the mate to the revolver that hung in its holster. It might be a good idea to take out that gun and practice with it, using his left hand.

At one time he had carried two guns. But as the years passed, he had found that one was enough for his needs. And so he had put away his other gun, wrapping it in an oiled cloth against rust. He would get it out, hang it in its shellbelt at his side, and begin his practice with it.

A stirring to one side made him turn and glance at the girl. Fay was sitting up, tousle-headed with sleep, her cheeks flushed.

"I smelled coffee," she murmured.

"Sure. Breakfast's about ready."

She threw off the blanket and stood up, stretching. Her clothes were rumpled—Kinniston thought she looked more like a gamin than ever—but there was a beauty to her that tugged at him.

They ate their breakfast and then Kinniston went and lifted his warbag, taking out his second Colt. It was worn with use, but it was clean and would function as it always had. He slung the heavy belt about his lean hips and bent to tie the thongs to his left thigh.

Fay watched his movements with wide eyes. When he noticed her, he said slowly, "Right arm's just about useless now. I'll make do with my left."

"Can you?"

His left hand dropped and lifted so swiftly that the girl gasped. The gun was in his hand miraculously fast.

"How did you do that? Get it out so fast, I mean?"

"Spent years making sure I could." His eyes touched the Colt. "Glad I did, now." He shook his head. "I've lost some speed, though. Have to do some practicing."

"Nobody could be any faster."

He chuckled. "I could. But I'll have to spend some time at it, get back my coordination."

With Fay seated on a rock staring, he spent the next two hours merely drawing the gun. His right hand hung at his side, but it was the left which darted downward. He did not fire the Colt, there was no need for that; he would shoot it when he was satisfied with his speed of hand.

They hunted, afterward, with Fay keeping close on his heels. They moved between the big trees, savoring the crispness of the air, and they moved like Indians, careful of where they stepped, avoiding the dried branches and twigs on the ground.

They did not speak. Fay could tell from the way Kinniston acted that he wanted no sound to disturb the silence of this high place, nothing that might alert a browsing deer.

They saw no deer, but Kinniston shot two big rabbits.

With them in hand, he turned back toward their camp. Now he walked more casually, not caring where he stepped. Fay went beside him, occasionally glancing up into his sunbrowned face.

"You like this sort of living, don't you?" she asked after a time. "Living under the sky, hunting your food. Not caring for the rest of the world."

"Always been a loner."

"Why?"

His eyes touched her intent face. "Never cared much for men."

"And—women?"

"Nor them, either."

When they came to a little stream, Kinniston knelt down, pushed up his sleeve, and was about to smear mud on it when Fay scooped up a handful of the wet muck and smeared it over his forearm, very gently.

He watched her, eyes intent.

"Does it hurt?" she asked.

"Not much, not any more."

"It looks as though it does."

He smiled wryly. "I've been hurt worse."

They sat there while the mud on his arm dried. It was pleasant, with the water gurgling at their feet, the wind filled with the fragrance of growing things. That wind blew Fay's golden hair around, adding to her gamin look.

"Wash off your arm," she said, "I'll put more mud on it."

He did as she asked and when she had plastered his

arm again, they sat on the bank and eyed each other.

"What am I going to do with you?" he asked suddenly.

She stared at him, and it seemed to Kinniston that something in her crumpled at his words. Her blue eyes seemed very big. She swallowed.

"Ca-can't I come with you?" she asked weakly.

His eyes moved from hers, to stare at the trees on the other side of the stream. "Not used to having a girl around."

"Am I—so much trouble?"

He squirmed. How could he make her understand that his was a blood trail? That he was intent only on one thing: vengeance on the men who had shot him down? A girl like Fay Mercer would not understand that, nor would she understand the fact that there was no place in his life for a woman.

Kinniston shook his head. "No, you're no trouble. But—"

"Go on. Say it."

"When you first saw me, I was on my way into Wardance to kill two men. I can't take you in with me. And if anything happened to me, where would that leave you?"

"I got no place to go."

His eyes swung back. "You got your ranchland."

"And what's that? The house is gone, burned down. The cows we had—well, I suppose the men who burned down the ranch took them. Or will."

Kinniston sighed. He was not going to get involved in this girl's troubles. By rights he ought to get rid of her, go on into Wardance by himself and begin asking questions. That letter he had found on Red Patsy had told him his long search was near an end.

If Tom Yancey and Dutch Korman were in Wardance. . . .

He looked again at the girl, who was watching him closely. She depended on him for her life. He understood that. Those men who had killed her father and brother might be looking for her even now. She had nobody to look to for help but him.

He rose to his feet.

"Come on. Let's go cook these rabbits."

Fay sighed and joined him, walking beside him silently. Her lips quivered and she fought the tears that struggled to flood her eyes. What was going to happen to her? Was Abel Kinniston going to abandon her? Would she wake up one morning and find him gone?

She trudged on, shoulders slumping.

Gib Young stared across his big mahogany desk at Luther Kesselring. His paralyzed cheek was hurting him again and so he rubbed it even as he considered what the big German had told him.

"Two bodies," he muttered.

"Just two. The town marshal nodded.

"Both male."

"The girl got away. I have the feeling she was helped. Horse tracks. Somebody came up on the house when it was burning and took her away. The horse was carrying double, its tracks were a little deeper when it went away."

"So. Somebody knows. You follow those tracks?"

"For a little while. They didn't lead to any of the other ranches. They headed straight for the Lances."

Gib Young sighed. "Luther, we got to find her, kill her."

The big blond man scowled. "I'm not much of a one to gun down a girl, Gib."

"I'll send French John and Bobby Cranford."

Luther Kesselring shifted uneasily. "Think they can do the job?"

Gib Young stared at him. "Why not?"

"Just thinking. Night or two ago you came into Wardance with some story about a stranger who'd buffaloed the Kid. If it was that same man—"

He let his words trail off as Gib Young stiffened. "By God, you may be right. Never thought about him." He scowled more blackly, then rasped, "Who is he, Dutch? He scared Bobby just by looking at him."

"Who knows? Some wandering stranger. But he won't scare French John."

"No. All right, I'll send them. And thanks, Dutch. I'm glad now I sent you out there to have a look."

The big German rose to his feet, putting his hat over his thick yellow hair. He paused a moment, staring downward. He sighed, then muttered, "If they can't handle him, we got trouble, Tom. Might have to go after him myself."

"We'll see. I'll send Crow along with them to make sure they find them. Crow's the best tracker I ever saw."

"He won't fight, you know. What I mean is, he won't take sides. He'll just stand there and watch."

"Hoping the palefaces will kill each other. I know. I don't expect him to fight, just find them."

Gib Young sat quietly as the other man left the room. He waited until bootfalls told him French John and Bobby Cranford were coming. Then he rose and began to pace the room.

As they came in, he swung around. "Got a little job for you boys. That Mercer girl is still alive. Some stranger carried her off, the other night."

Bobby Cranford felt some of his tension ease out of him. He let his lips slide into a grin. "I can handle her."

"You'll put lead in her, that's what you'll do," snapped Young. "You think I want her alive, to tell the law what we did?"

French John nodded. He was a lean man with black hair and glistening black eyes. He wore a beat-up hat and his shirt and levis were worn and dirty. He rolled a smoke as he stood there, and when he had taken a puff, he chuckled.

"Better let me handle the girl. Bobby's sweet on her."

"You settle that between you. I'm giving you Crow so he can find them for you. I want that girl dead, you hear? Longer she stays alive, the more worried I am. I don't like to worry."

French John smiled coldly, "Then don't. We can handle this."

Bobby Cranford did not like the fact that Fay Mercer was to die. He hungered for that girl, and there was a tightness in his belly. Yet he was afraid of Gib Young; he did not dare say anything. He followed French John out into the yard and they walked side by side toward their horses.

"Don't like the idea of killing the girl," Bobby muttered.

French John stopped and looked at him. There was amusement in him. "Kid, forget it. There are plenty of girls. The boss wants all that land along Butterwood Creek. What's a girl compared to that?"

"Just the same, I don't like it."

"You want to pull out and let me handle it?"

Bobby Cranford knew what would happen if he did that. He would be finished here at Fencepost. In Wardance, too. Gib Young might not even let him live. Maybe French John was right. What was one girl, compared to what he had here?

"I'm coming," he said slowly.

French John grinned coldly. "I'll kill the girl, Bobby. You won't have to worry about that. You just do your job when we find the man who took her away."

Bobby felt better. It didn't bother him to gun down a man. His step grew lighter as he walked, and when he swung up into the kak he was smiling.

Little Crow came to join them after a time, mounted on a pinto horse. He carried a knife at his belt, and a battered old Winchester was in the sheath under his right leg. His black eyes touched the two men who waited for him.

He didn't like either of these men. They were killers for money. Little Crow did not object to killing; it was the money part that bothered him. If a man killed another out of hate or for his honor, that was one thing. But just for money? There was a sneer on his lips as he trotted his horse ahead of theirs.

"We're headin' for Triangle," French John said.

Little Crow did not bother to answer. He would track whoever it was that they wanted tracked, but he would not lift a hand in the fighting. Let the palefaces kill each other if they wanted to. He would do his job, then stand aside while the fighting went on.

They headed out across the grasslands toward Triangle.

For five days, Kinniston rested.

As those days passed he was discovering that he was growing used to having Kay Mercer around. It was pleasant seeing her pretty face in the morning, watching her move so gracefully from their campfire to the food she was preparing. It was enjoyable having her walk with him or sit beside the stream bank and smear his forearm with mud.

His arm was healing, slowly but steadily. Of course he wasn't able to use it yet; it was still too stiff. But new flesh was forming on it, and in a few weeks it would be as good as ever.

Meanwhile he practiced his draw with his left. Hour after hour, day after day, he stood and made his move, lifting out the gun. The old skill was coming back to him; the memory of those long years when he had yanked out his gun again and again with his left hand was returning.

Even now his left hand was almost as fast as his right had ever been. And yet he was not satisfied. Daily he stood and worked at his task, calmly and patiently, aware that his very life might depend upon the speed of that left hand and arm.

Fay was always with him, staring at him, as quiet as a frightened animal. Her blue eyes watched him closely; she seemed almost afraid that he would vanish before her eyes. In time Kinniston grew used to having her tagging along with him.

Yet he worried about her. It was not right to subject a girl to these hardships. She ought to be somewhere with a roof over her head, with a proper bed to sleep in of nights. He was used to living under the sky. She was not.

She made no complaint, of course. Indeed, she was forever smiling, always cheerful. Only when he looked away did a touch of wistfulness come into her face.

Yet there grew up in them a sense of camaraderie, a sharing of this carefree life. It was Fay who gathered the firewood, who cooked the meals. It was Fay, too, who cleaned the animals he shot, who skinned and gutted them and cut away the finer portions of the meat to be cooked or smoked. She made the biscuits and the coffee.

Kinniston taught her to hunt, to walk across ground where her footfalls would make no sound to alert the animals they hunted. She had fired a rifle before, though only at targets her brother had set up for her.

She shot a deer once, with Kinniston at her elbow watching. Her eyes misted with tears when she saw the deer drop, and she choked back a sob.

Kinniston saw, and smiled grimly. "We're out of food," he told her. "It was our lives or that of the deer."

She nodded, but she didn't seem to feel any better about it.

When they had been in their hideout for more than a week, Kinniston said, "We got to go back to Carbine."

She looked at him, eyes big. "Why?"

"Running out of coffee. Flour, too. Got to lay in a fresh supply."

He had made up his mind. He was going to leave her there, in that little town. She would be safe enough. He was going back into the high hills and live as he had always lived, alone, until his right arm was healed. Then he would set out for Wardance, to find Tom Yancey and Dutch Korman.

He could not meet her eyes. In them he would see reproach and worry. She was a smart girl; she would guess what he meant to do.

"I could stay here, couldn't I?" she asked.

Kinniston only shook his head.

They rode into Carbine in late afternoon, side by side. Fay had been silent for all of that ride; it was as though she knew what he meant to do and could find no words to express her worry. Kinniston, too, had spoken no words. He was naturally a quiet man, but now there was a strange guilt inside him.

What would she do when he had left her? Oh, he would leave some money with her; he could not abandon her without funds. If she were smart she would ride back to what was left of Triangle and try to make a go of it.

They came up before the hitching bar and Kinniston swung down from the kak. Fay was already on the ground, staring at him with those big blue eyes that seemed to eat into him.

"Come along," he muttered. "We'll hire you a room for the night. We won't go back until tomorrow."

"And you? Won't you sleep in a room?"

Her voice was little more than a whisper, yet it struck into him like a knife.

"I'll sleep outside. Used to it."

Her head bowed and her shoulders rounded. Yet she walked with him into the hotel and stood close by as he asked for a room and then gave her the pen to sign the register.

"Go upstairs and rest," he muttered. "Take a bath. If you need some clothes, I'll try and rustle them up."

"You won't find any girl clothes in this place," she muttered.

"I'll look around while you lie down."

He turned on a heel and walked from the hotel, heading for the general store. He needed flour and bacon; he would buy as much as he could carry, then be on his way.

He had not asked to become involved in Fay Mercer's life. It had happened; he could scarcely have left her to die in that fire. But was that a reason why he should be saddled with her for the rest of his life?

He made his purchases, carried out the gunnysack toward the Nez Perce horse. His hands busied themselves with strapping on the sack. Then he swung up into the saddle and nudged the big stallion with his toe.

He cantered out of town, heading for the high hills.

chapter 6

Kinniston rode for close to half an hour before he pulled back on the reins and turned in the saddle, looking back the way he had come. There was a scowl on his face and uneasiness in the pit of his stomach.

Fay Mercer was alone back there. Without a friend, with no money. What would happen to her, without his being there to help?

He squirmed in the kak, feeling guilty.

He was abandoning her. There was no other word for it. In all his life he had never felt this guilty. Before now, all he had had to be concerned about was himself.

"Damn," he muttered.

He swung the Nez Perce horse around and sent it back toward Carbine at a gallop. He could not leave her alone, without funds, without a friend. As he rode, his uneasiness fled away, and he was surprised at the warm feeling inside him.

Kinniston grinned. He was saddled with the girl, that was all there was to it. Might as well admit it. After his arm was healed he could decide what to do about her. But for now, he was going to get her and take her back with him to the high hills. There she would be safe.

The town loomed before him, and he saw two horses

tied to the hitching post before the saloon. Kinniston slowed the headlong gallop of the stallion at sight of them. Two punchers off the ranches? A couple of outlaws, stopping by for some liquor and maybe some food?

No matter. He would get Fay and be out of Carbine in a matter of minutes. Nobody was going to stop him.

He reined up, looped the reins over the post, and moved toward the saloon. His hand hit the swinging doors and he stepped to one side instantly, while his eyes became accustomed to the darkness of the big room.

Two men were at the bar. With something of surprise, he recognized Bobby Cranford. Ah, yes. The man with him was French John.

It was Bobby Cranford who turned to stare at him. The glass in his hand slipped from his fingers and clattered on the floor.

French John felt the tension in his companion and swung around. His face was hard, lean, and there was a puzzlement in it, as though he were searching his memory for the identity of this man who stood before him.

"That's him," whispered Bobby Cranford.

The barkeep was frozen, his eyes moving from Kinniston to the two men who stood as though made of stone.

"Kinniston," whispered French John, disbelief strong in his throat.

This was the man who had taken Fay Mercer out of the burning Triangle building. French John knew it as though a voice had spoken inside him. He tensed.

Gib Young wanted this man dead.

His hand flashed downward. At the same time, Bobby Cranford went for his own gun. Kinniston did not move his right arm. But his left flashed downward and up and the sounds of his two shots were almost as one. They crashed loudly in the big room, seeming to echo from the walls.

French John buckled, his gun in his hand but pointing floorward. Then the gun fell from his nerveless fingers and clattered on the floor. Bobby Cranford went back a step until his spine was against the bar. Then he slid downward, slowly, his eyes glazing over.

French John pitched onto the floor and lay there.

Kinniston glanced at the bartender. "They went for their guns," he said flatly.

The barkeep nodded. He had not seen Kinniston move that left arm, but the gun had been in his hand and it had erupted twice. He glanced over the edge of the bar at the two bodies.

"They made their play," he agreed.

He knew French John as a fast gun, and he had heard tales about Bobby Cranford. Yet they lay here as mute evidence that this unknown man before him was greased lightening.

There was a clatter of shoes on the staircase and Fay Mercer burst into the room. Her eyes lighted up at sight of Kinniston, and then she stared at the two bodies. She gasped when she recognized Bobby Cranford.

"You ready to travel?" Kinniston asked harshly.

Fay nodded, still staring down at the bodies. "Wha-what did they want?" she asked.

"Laying for me."

She shook her head. "They didn't know where you were." She turned and stared at the big man in the black clothes. "They were hunting me. They weren't satisfied to kill my pa and my brother. They wanted to kill me, too."

She shivered.

Kinniston eyed her a moment, then nodded. "Makes sense. With you dead, anybody could claim your ranch. But who? Who sent them?"

"They work for Fencepost. Gib Young's ranch."

"Come on, let's be moving."

"But—those bodies. . . ."

"The barkeep will bury them."

He waited as she moved toward him. His eyes touched the bartender, who nodded. Kinniston reached into a pocket, brought out a gold coin and tossed it through the air. The bartender caught it with a sidewise motion of his hand.

"Bury them," Kinniston said.

Then he urged Fay out of the swinging doors ahead of him and moved with her around the side of the building to where he had left her horse. She walked beside him with lowered head, saying nothing.

Only when they were riding out of the little town did she murmur, "I thought you'd left me."

He turned and looked at her and now, for the first time, he saw that her eyes were red as though she had been weeping. Well, he didn't blame her for that; it must have been pretty hard to take when she first realized he had gone off and left her.

"Changed my mind," he growled.

"Why?" she asked, with a woman's directness.

What could he tell her? That she had gnawed inside him all during that half hour when he had been riding away from Carbine? That something inside him had mocked at him, had pestered him until he turned the Nez Perce horse around and rode back to Carbine?

"Missed you."

She hestitated an instant, and then she smiled. The smile transfigured her face, made it beautiful.

"I thought you were never coming back. And then

I saw Bobby Cranford and French John ride in and I knew—"

She swallowed. They had been after her. If they had not paused at the bar, if they had come in and asked questions and learned that she was in an upstairs room, she would not be alive right now.

"We got a far piece to ride," he said.

He led the way on the big stallion and her horse came close behind him. They went upward, always upward between the trembling aspen close beside the brooks they passed, and the fir trees that grew so thickly. Overhead the sky was a pale blue, the sun was like a big yellow ball. A wind came up after a time and blew against them.

When they were almost at their camp, Fay asked, "Do you think they'll send anyone else after me?"

Kinniston smiled grimly. "Let them."

She eyed him wonderingly. "You aren't afraid of them?"

He turned in the saddle to look back at her. "They're just men. Men can die when they crowd me too close. I don't like to be crowded."

She urged the pony to a faster trot until she came up to Kinniston. Like that, side by side, they moved on through the firs, upward toward their camp.

Little Crow trotted his pinto across the grasslands. In his hand he held a rope. Attached to that rope were the reins of two horses. The Indian was smiling under the shadow of his battered old hat with the single feather thrusting upward from the sweat-stained band.

French John and the Kid were dead. He himself had helped to bury them, once that black-clad man had moved out of Carbine with the girl. He had not seen them killed, he had been out back, hunkered down and chewing on a bit of meat. He did not like the liquor that the white men drank, and so he was content to stay out of any saloon they entered.

He chuckled. He had heard the shots, though. Just two of them. He had frozen at their sound, believing they had killed the girl they were hunting. Yet he had not moved. He had remained that way until he had heard the sound of hooves. Then he had run to the edge of the building and stared after a black-clad man and the yellow-haired girl he knew to be Fay Mercer.

Only then had he gone into the saloon.

Two shots. One for John French, one for the Kid. And they were both dead. They had gone for their guns, the barkeep told him. But the man they faced had gunned them down.

Who was he? What man could take both French John and the Kid in a fair fight? It was a puzzle that Little Crow pondered over as his pinto trotted onward.

Not that it was any concern of his. Let the palefaces kill each other. He did his job, he kept aloof from their quarrels, their antagonisms. Enough for him that he got his pay and that he did the jobs Gib Young gave him.

The bossman would not like the story he had to tell. He would stroke his cheek and his eyes would get hard and wary, and this would send a thrill of pleasure down Little Crow's spine. He did not like Gib Young.

When he came into the ranchyard, he swung down from the pinto and moved toward the ranch house. The boss would be furious at his news, and this made the Indian chuckle.

Young was behind his desk as he entered. He looked up and then frowned. "Back already? Is the girl dead?"

"No. But French John and the Kid are."

Gib Young came up off his chair, eyes wide. He

stared into the impassive face of the Indian and his thoughts ran riot.

"Man killed them."

Gib Young sank back into the chair and stared. "One man?" he asked incredulously. "*One man* beat them both?"

Little Crow shrugged. "So the barkeep said. They went for their guns. The man drew and shot them both. Took only two bullets, one for each of them."

The seated man let out a long breath. His eyes were still wide, filled with disbelief. "I don't believe it," he said at last, very slowly. "Did you see it?"

"I was out back. But the bartender saw it. He told me what happened."

"Who? Who was it?"

"French John knew him. He said a name."

Gib Young stared at the Indian. What man could have beaten both French John and Bobby Cranford? He didn't believe that one man could have killed them both in a fair fight.

"He got them from behind," he said harshly.

Little Crow shook his head. "Face to face. They went for their guns. So did the other one. He got them both, one bullet for each."

Gib Young rubbed his cheek. "What name?" he asked in a hoarse whisper.

Little Crow shrugged. "The bartender not sure. He said it sounded like Kinniston."

"*Kinniston!*"

Gib Young came off the chair to stand bent over behind his big desk, eyes wide and staring into the face of the Indian. He didn't know it, but his face had grown much paler.

He said softly, "Kinniston is dead."

Little Crow shrugged. "I not know. I see him ride

off with the girl. He wears black. All over, black."

Gib Young sagged. Could it be? They had left Abel Kinniston stretched out dead, back there along the Santa Fe trail. How many years ago had it been? Two? Three? Ah, he was a fool. It couldn't be Kinniston. It had been someone dressed like him.

Ah, but who? What man possessed the speed of hand in making a draw to get both French John and the Kid in a fair fight? There was nobody. Well, maybe Dutch Korman could. But nobody else.

Nobody—but Kinniston.

Yes, Kinniston could have done it, if he were alive.

The bartender had muttered a name. French John had spoken that name, and he knew that French John knew Kinniston. If he had not made a mistake—

His hand waved Little Crow away, wanting to be alone with his thoughts. They were not pleasant ones. He thought back, and it came to him that Red Patsy, to whom he had written long ago, had never showed up here at Fencepost.

Could Kinniston have met up with him? Killed him?

He stood and came around the desk, striding up and down, the thoughts whirling in his head. If it really were Kinniston, if by some trick of the devil he had lived after being shot down, if he were on his trail and that of Dutch as well, he would have to do something about it.

Otherwise, all this that he had stolen by cards and added to with violence, would float away in a cloud of gunsmoke. If Kinniston were alive, he was trailing him, Gib Young. Well, not Gib Young, but Tom Yancey. Kinniston didn't know the name he was using now. There was that much to be thankful for.

He walked out on the porch. First thing he had to do was warn Dutch. He didn't want the blond man to be caught by surprise—not if he had to go up against Abel Kinniston. Yancey moved out across the yard and called to Little Crow to saddle his horse.

In moments, he was galloping along the road to Wardance.

Dutch Korman was walking down the street when he saw Gib Young on the lathered horse. He stopped walking and waited, his eyes going over this man who had been his friend for a long time. There was something eating in Gib Young, and eating hard.

He drew up his horse in a flutter of dust and stared down at the German. "We got to talk, Dutch."

The marshal stared up into the taut, pallid face that looked down at him. Tom Yancey was not a man to panic, unless there was a damn good reason for panic. There was no such reason as far as Dutch Korman knew.

"My place," he said slowly, and turned to lead the way.

When they were in the living room of the house where Luther Kesselring lived, Gib Young dropped into a chair. He stared straight before him, and inside him he was cold.

The marshal said, "You rode that horse to a stagger, getting here. What's so important?"

"Kinniston. He's alive."

Dutch Korman froze, his hands, which had been in the act of rolling a cigarette, very still. He knew a moment of panic, then told himself he was a fool. Even if Abel Kinniston were alive—a fact he doubted very much—there was no need to sit frozen with fear. He cleared his throat.

"Who says so?"

"Little Crow. Kinniston gunned down French John and the Kid, both at the same time. Seems French John knew him."

Korman lit the cigarette he had made, drew in on it and let out smoke. "I'll believe it when I see him. You say French John is dead? And the Kid?"

"Over in Carbine."

He told his friend what the Indian had related, adding, "Kinniston always wore black. The man who shot them down was all in black. And French John muttered his name."

Korman shook his head. "Looks like I'm going to have to go after him myself."

Gib Young glanced up. "Don't be a fool. You think you could take Kinniston, man to man?"

"He'd have to hump himself to beat me."

"Kinniston isn't human, Dutch. He's a man with the soul of a wolf. A lone wolf. Nobody's ever beat his gunhand. Nobody ever will."

"He's got you spooked, that's for sure."

"I look facts in the face. Kinniston is a manhunter. He's made his living killing people. Always in a fair fight, I grant you. And now he's after us."

"Hasn't found us yet."

Gib Young rose and walked back and forth. There was fear inside him, a fear he did not conceal. Here he had everything a man could want: a ranch, plenty of money, herds of cattle, a reputation as a good man. Now he was about to lose it all, including his life.

The face he lifted toward his friend was strained. "Dutch, what are we going to do?"

"Go on living. Keep at it, just as we have been doing. If Kinniston wants to come after us, why let him."

In a soft voice, Young asked, "And when he does—what then?"

"We shoot him down like a mad dog. You think he can take both of us? Together?"

Gib Young thought for a moment. "Maybe not.

Might be I'm like a calf bawling for its mother. It could be the surprise of learning that Kinniston isn't dead."

"If he isn't."

Young chuckled. "Yeah. You could be right. Just because that man was wearing black clothes and—no. It wasn't just the black clothes. It was because he gunned down both French John and the Kid face to face."

"If it was face to face."

The ranchman shook his head. "Little Crow don't lie. No reason for him to. He told me the barkeep said it was a fair fight, and I can't think of any reason for the barkeep to lie. *Somebody* got them both."

"Then we wait for him to make his play for us, if that's what he's going to do. Go back to Fencepost, Tom. Keep your eyes peeled, but say nothing. I'll maybe ride over to Carbine and talk to that bartender. Could be he'll tell me something he didn't tell Crow."

Gib Young nodded. "A good idea. Crow said he had a blond girl with him. That'd be Fay Mercer."

The marshal nodded. "I'll get him to describe her, too. If I feel it really is the Mercer girl, we can make plans." He began to build another cigarette, eyes thoughtful. "What gets me is, if that's Kinniston, what's he doing out there in the Lances? Why don't he come on in to Wardance?"

Young chuckled. "He's got the girl with him."

Kesselring shook his head. "Kinniston—if it is Kinniston—isn't that kind of man. He don't fool with women. He's always been a loner. I'm sort of surprised he keeps the girl with him."

"He took her out of the burning ranch house. What else was he going to do with her?"

The marshal blew smoke out slowly. "I'd better dust over to Carbine first thing in the morning. The more you tell me, the less I like what I hear."

"You be careful, Dutch. Don't go up against Kinniston all by yourself. We can handle him, if we put our minds to it. But together, not one by one."

"You may be right. Come on. Walk over to the Prairie Queen. Have a drink. Let Ginny see you. Been a while since you've spent some time with her."

Gib Young shrugged. "Why not? Might do me good. My nerves aren't what they usually are. Maybe I do need some quieting down."

"Trust Ginny for that. Come along."

They went out into the night and walked side by side along the street. They could hear the voices of the miners in the Desert Rose, the sounds of a tinny piano from the Glory Hand.

All this belonged to him, Gib Young reflected. This was his town, those were his people in the saloons. Every dollar they spent was credited to his accounts. He was a rich man, and around here his word was law.

He would not give all this up. He would not let Abel Kinniston take it away from him by shooting him. He must think of a way to save his skin. No matter what else happened, that was the important thing.

As they moved into the Prairie Queen, he saw Ginny stand up and wave to him. He stroke forward to meet her, his worry dropping away.

chapter seven

For two weeks Abel Kinniston had lazed away the long days. He had hunted in the high hills, he had brought down several deer and once a bull elk, a golden giant which took him three days to dismember and bring back to their camp.

Always, Fay went with him on his hunts; she was like his shadow, moving as he moved, stopping instantly when he froze at sight of an animal. Her eyes studied him as though she sought to discover why it was he wanted so much to be alone.

Now as they feasted on elk steaks, she asked, "How long do you intend hiding up here?"

His eyes touched her face. "Until my right arm heals."

"It's all better. I've seen you use it often enough. You know what I think?"

"You might as well tell me."

"I think you're just wasting time. Because you have me with you, and you don't know what to do with me."

"Could be."

He was the most exasperating man! He rarely spoke to her, and then only when she talked to him and he could hardly avoid speech. Always he was deferential to her, he considered her comfort and her safety before his own. But she was a burden to him. She could see that from the way he acted.

She considered him now, beneath lowered eyelids.

"You could take me to one of the other ranches," she said slowly. At his sharp glance, she shrugged. "Of course, Gib Young is going to put them out of business, too—but that's no concern of yours."

She waited, watching his face. When he did not speak, she asked. "Is it? You don't care what happens to anybody, do you? Just as long as you can go on your way."

"Gave up caring a long time ago," he said slowly, pushing a few more sticks on the fire. "Got me one thing to do, and after that—"

His wide shoulders lifted and fell in a shrug.

"Wouldn't hurt you to help those people."

"What people?"

"The ones Gib Young is trying to run off their ranchland, just as he did to Pop and Benjie. Burn down their ranch houses, shoot them down like mad dogs, and then take over everything they've worked for."

"No concern of mine."

"Why?" she flared. "You're a human being. You ought to care what happens to other people."

"Told you. I got me two men to kill."

"Can't that wait? Can't you use those guns of yours to help somebody first? Help those other ranchers, let them get to be able to hold their heads high. Help them to be able to walk into Wardance and order the flour and bacon and the tools they need."

The fire flared up, its red flames tinting Kinniston's cheekbones. They touched his eyes, made them seem to flame.

"You mean they're not able to buy anything in Wardance?"

"Not with Gib Young running the town."

He considered what she was telling him. Always in the past he had sold his guns to men who needed them. Never had he given their use away for anything but hard cash which he had put in his pocket. A thought touched his mind, and he turned more fully to run his eyes over her intent face.

"This Gib Young you keep talking about. What manner of man is he?"

"Hard. He reaches out for everything. Won his ranch in a poker game and the man he won it from was found dead a little later. It was supposed to be suicide, but Shad Tremaine—the man he'd won the ranch from—wasn't the sort to kill himself."

Kinniston shifted his position, then asked, "What does Young look like?"

Fay shrugged. "I guess you could call him handsome. He's lean and dangerous and I've heard tell he's an excellent poker player. He has a cheek that pains him at times and—"

She gasped as he reached out and caught her wrist in his big hand. "Does he have black hair and black eyes?"

She nodded dumbly, startled at the fury that seemed to convulse this man beside her.

He drew back and released her wrist. She began to rub it, still staring at him.

"Does he have a close friend in that town? A big, blond man who is quite a gunman?"

"That would be Luther Kesselring. He's the town marshal. Gib Young made him marshal when he won the Fencepost and started taking over the town."

Kinniston stood up and walked back and forth, head down, but his eyes glittered and Fay saw that there was a wild excitement eating in him. He reminded her of a stalking wolf, lean and dangerous. His hands fell to his gunbutts and clenched tightly about them.

"Gib Young and Luther Kesselring," Kinniston whispered. "It could be, it could be."

A man could change his name easily enough. He did not find it so easy to change the habits of a lifetime. The same cheek that used to pain Tom Yancey might be the one that annoyed Gib Young. And where Tom Yancey was, he was certain that he would find Dutch Korman. Was Dutch Korman now Luther Kesselring? He fought to conquer the wild excitement flooding him.

Was he coming to the end of the trail at last?

From what Fay Mercer had told him, Yancey and Korman had the town of Wardance in their hip pockets. Might not be so easy to walk up to them and start shooting. He would be smarter to play this game close to the vest.

He swung about and looked at the girl.

"Tomorrow we ride down out of the hills. We'll go visit these ranches you mentioned."

Kay felt her heart begin to pound. "You do want to be rid of me."

He shook his head. "No. We aren't going for that reason. You said these ranchers can't get what they need in Wardance. I figure it might be a good idea to ride into town with them and make certain they're served what they need."

She eyed him warily. "It'll mean gunplay, maybe."

His hands touched the handles of his Colts. "I'm ready."

Fay pressed it. "Are you sure?"

His hands blurred and when she looked again, she saw the big Peacemakers in his hands. She cried out in surprise.

"Your arm is better. I—I never even saw that draw."

"Been practicing lately. I'll be all right. Maybe my arm is still a little sore, but it doesn't bother me." His eyes went over the girl, and he smiled. "You go get some sleep now. I want to be away from here early in the morning."

She moved away toward the little windbreak he had made for her and lay down, drawing the blanket over her and then rolling up in it. Yet she did not sleep. She went on staring at Kinniston where he paced before the fire.

With a man like this as her husband, she could be a very happy girl, she thought. Of course, he never looked at her as a man looked at a woman. To him she was just an inconvenience, a burden which he had assumed and couldn't wait to be rid of. Fay kicked a leg angrily. Was he made of stone? Didn't he have a heart? No. Most definitely, he did not.

She turned over so that her back was toward him.

Kinniston roused her when the sun was just peeping over the Lances. He had already shaved, she saw, he had brushed his clothes and was ready to ride. Fay sighed and slid out of the blanket, smelling frying bacon.

They ate seated across the fire from each other. There seemed to be a repressed eagerness in Abel Kinniston, a deliberate muffling of the energies that ran so strongly inside him. Yet he lingered a little over the coffee.

"You sure you can stay at one of the ranches down on the flatlands?" he asked.

She nodded glumly. "Yes, The Willises will take me in. That's the Bar W ranch. There are some others, too, along the creek, ranches that Gib Young wants to own. Someday he will, too. The small ranchers can't fight him."

"All they need is somebody to show them how."

113

"You could do it, Abel," she announced eagerly. "You know all about that sort of thing."

He stared off into the distance. "We'll see."

Something inside her told Fay not to push right now. The mere fact that this man would even consider helping those little ranchers was a triumph of sorts. Fay smiled to herself and then rose to carry their plates and the tin cup to the mountain brook to wash them. Behind her, Kinniston was already breaking camp, making packs for their mounts.

In minutes they were ready. Fay swung up into her saddle, watched as Kinniston ran his eyes around their camp. Then he lifted upward onto the Nez Perce horse and touched it with a toe.

They rode down out of the timberland, moving steadily. Here and there were great rocks piled high, one upon the other, as though tumbled about by a giant hand, while all about them rose the tall pines, and a stream of water gurgled over bottom stones. It was a wild country, remote from any human habitation, where the deer and bighorn sheep would be more at home than any man.

Fay eyed this man who rode beside her. He seemed at home here, she thought. He was like a part of this mountain, he was one with the wind that whispered as it moved between the firs and the pines, one with the brook as it danced along its course. There was a wildness about him, but it was a restrained wildness that made it much like this wilderness through which they moved.

It came to her that he was more at home here than he had been at the ranch house, when she had fed him supper. He was used to these lonely trials, to the emptiness of the land around him. A man such as this would never make a husband, she thought gloomily.

Now the firs and lodgepole pines were giving way to junipers and cottonwoods, with a scattering of box elder. Always, Kinniston rode easily in the kak, almost as though he were a part of this mountainside. From time to time he would rein up and send his gaze around him, sometimes standing in the stirrups for a better view.

Fay watched him, copying his movements. She halted when he did, rested in the saddle as he did, and she looked where he stared.

"You expecting trouble?" she asked at last.

"All the time," he said.

He was as wary as a wild creature. She was confident that nothing escaped his eyes. When a bear lumbered out from a little copse, he noted its movements. Where an eagle flew high overhead, his upward glance grew aware of it. He did not pull back on the reins, nor did he reach for a gun when a lynx snarled from a tall rock to one side of the trail. Kinniston, she told herself, was in his element here. He was a part of it.

They came down onto the flatlands and now he looked at her. "You know how to get to this Bar W ranch?"

When she nodded, he let her take the lead. Like that, they went out onto the grasslands and rode for hours. They sighted some steers, here and there, and Kinniston shifted in the kak, eyeing them. Fay wondered what he was thinking. They were good steers; the feed and water on this range was good and steers like that would grow fat.

Once she pulled up until he came beside her. Fay jerked her head at the steers. "This is good grazeland. Its rich, and there's plenty of grass. Also water."

"A man could make a fortune on land like this." he agreed.

Fay smiled coldly. "If he were allowed to. Gib Young's the only one who does. Sometimes his riders come over here and shoot what cattle they find."

He looked his surprise. "Doesn't anybody object?"

"They do and they get shot." She didn't hide the bitterness in her. "Just the way Pop and Benjie got shot. Fencepost hires the killers and pays them well."

Kinniston listened, head bent. If Gib Young were really Tom Yancey, this would be the way he would act. Selfishly, considering only himself and his wants. Soon now, he would own this whole land. Probably he had already taken the steers that Fay Mercer owned and was rebranding them.

They rode on, and now they went stirrup to stirrup.

It was close to sundown when they reached the Bar W ranch house. Kinniston drew up and, when Fay glanced at him, shook his head.

"They don't know me," he said softly. "I don't like to ride in on a strange camp without announcing myself."

"They know me," Fay muttered, and nudged her horse to a trot.

A man came out from a barn and stood there, a rifle held loosely in his hands. Fay stood in the stirrups and waved her hand high above her head.

"It's Fay Mercer, Mr. Willis."

The rifle barrel lowered and the man moved forward. His right arm lifted in a wave. "Come on, Fay. Come ahead."

They trotted up to the barn and now Kinniston saw a young man rise from behind a woodpile, his rifle alert. He smiled grimly. Hell of a note when a man had to walk around his own home grounds with a rifle ready to use.

Fay was talking as she came down out of the saddle. "This here is Abel Kinniston, Mr. Willis. He dragged me out of the house when Gib Young's men killed Pop and Benjie and set fire to the ranch."

Jim Willis fixed Kinniston with hard eyes. "Heard about that. Thought they'd got you too, Fay." He hesitated, then said, "That was some weeks ago."

"Abel hurt his arm when he carried me out. We've been waiting for it to heal."

Jim Willis nodded. "You got here in time for supper. Reckon you might as well go indoors. Ma'll be glad to see you." His eyes touched Kinniston. "You too, mister."

Kinniston came down from the saddle and led his horse toward the water trough. The young man behind the woodpile watched him carefully. When the Nez Perce was finished, Kinniston unsaddled him and led him into the barn. He mixed oats and grain for his feed.

Young Joe Willis was beside him by that time, caring for Fay's pony. His eyes went over Kinniston, taking in the two guns hung low on his thighs.

"You siding Fay in this fight?" he asked.

Kinniston ran his eyes over the taut young face, then nodded. "I am. I mean to see her win it, too."

Joe Willis shook his head. "She won't win no fight. Neither will anybody else except Mr. Young. He'll take everything over one of these days. We're next on his list, I bet."

Abel Kinniston considered this young man, figuring his age at sixteen or seventeen. When he was that young he had been involved in that war with Homer Morrel and Toleman Ackley. Well, times were a little different, back then.

"You going to take it lying down?" he asked quietly.

Joe Willis straightened, flushing. "What can we do?"

"Fight, boy. Fight back. Kill a few men. It'll make a difference, you'll see."

"Paw don't hold with killin'."

Kinniston smiled coldly, then winked. "Time I had a little talk with him, then. Son, there's some people who don't talk any other language than killing. You want to get their respect, you kill a few people. It'll make them sit up and notice you."

He swung about and walked out of the barn with Joe Willis following close behind him and beginning to wonder if there might be some hope left, after all.

They moved into the ranch house, where a table was being laid with dishes. Fay was helping, but her eyes went instantly to Kinniston. She saw Jim Willis rise from the chair in which he had been sitting, frowning darkly.

Willis said, "Fay here has been telling me you gunned down French John and that Bobby Cranford."

When Kinniston nodded, the older man muttered, "That's bad news. Gib Young won't take that sittin' down."

"Hope he doesn't."

Willis smothered a gasp. "You know what that means? He'll send his riders to push us off our land, too."

"Figures. Young seems to be a greedy sort of man."

"But—"

Kinniston smiled gravely. "You thinking you're safe? Then you don't know men like Young. He'll hit you, one of these days, too. A man like Young is never satisfied until he owns everything."

"I don't like it."

"No more do I. But you have to face facts, Willis. According to what I hear, he won't let his stores in Wardance sell you food, or equipment you need to run your ranches right."

Jim Willis smothered a sigh. "He has us over a barrel. Not much we can do about it."

"Why not? There are other ranches around here. Small ones, but they got a right to exist. There's also some nesters, right? Farmers who've built on land that's free to all, but which Gib Young wants. He can drive you off one by one. He's already driven Fay off her land. He's burned down her ranch house and killed her father and brother."

Willis glanced at Fay, saw her watching from where she stood beside the big dinner table. He cleared his throat.

"Nothing we can do about it. We ain't as organized as Gib Young."

"You sure ought to be. You got enough, between the lot of you. Men who know how to fire a rifle, men who must have enough gumption to fight for what's rightfully theirs."

It was young Joe Willis who pushed into their talk, stepping forward and thrusting out his jaw pugnaciously.

"It ain't that we won't fight if we're attacked," he growled. "But everybody sits back and waits for the next man to make the move."

Kinniston eyed him a moment, then nodded. "You need anything in Wardance? Flour? Butter? Anything at all?"

A woman moved from the kitchen doorway where she had been standing. She was an older woman, with streaks of white hair in its brown. Her face was tanned, and held remnants of a former beauty. She dried her hands on her apron as she began to speak.

"You tell us what we can do, mister. If we ride into town, men who take the pay of Gib Young will shoot down my husband, my son. I can make do without bread, to keep them alive. They can patch up their broken tools. It's more important for them to stay alive than for us to be able to eat bread or biscuits."

"Is it, ma'am?" Kinniston asked softly. "Maybe that's what Fay's pa thought, and her brother. What did it get them except an attack in the night that killed them both? You think Young won't send his riders against you, now that he has their land?"

Clarissa Willis went white. Her lips quivered and tears came into her eyes. "You th-think he'll do that?"

"I do, ma'am. I've met men like Gib Young before. The only thing they can get through their thick skulls is hot lead. You show them you mean to fight, and they won't be so swift to reach out and grab what you've made your own."

"He's right, Ma," said Joe Willis. "I ain't so sure about what we can do, but he's right when he says that. The Bar W is next on Gib Young's list, I'll bet, now that he's taken over Triangle."

Fay said softly, "What can we do, Abel?"

Kinniston smiled faintly. "If I was ramroding this crew, I'd send Joe here off on a horse, first thing in the morning. I'd tell him to visit the other ranches and the nesters, tell them we're going to have a meeting here tomorrow. Tell them to make lists of what they need in Wardance, and come primed for shooting."

Jim Willis shook his head. There was worry on his face, but no fear. His eyes brooded at Kinniston, and then he nodded slowly.

"Maybe you're right, man. I've been thinking a lot lately, and I'm admitting that Gib Young might not have to send any men onto Bar W land. If he waits long enough we'll probably all starve to death."

Young Joe growled, "I vote we do what Kinniston says. I'll ride at sunup. I know the nesters, I know the ranchers. They'll listen to me. They're right in the same boat we're in. They'll probably starve to death too, unless they can lay hands on supplies they'll be needin'."

Clarissa Willis glanced from her son to her husband. Her lips tightened, and she snapped, "I vote right along with Joe. It's time we got out of our shell and fought for what we know is our rights."

Jim Willis glanced at his wife, his face softening, losing some of its bitter hardness. "You think so, mother? All right. I'll vote along with you." He drew a deep breath. "I kind of hanker for some of those biscuits you used to bake. I'll even fight for them."

Kinniston said swiftly, "You let me do the fighting. All I want is your wagons out in front come tomorrow, with all the men you can get carrying guns. I promise you that you'll get what you need in Wardance."

Clarissa Willis clapped her hands together. "That's settled, then. Come on, sit down. We'll have dinner on the table in a jiffy."

They ate and they talked, an as she ran her eyes around the table, Fay Mercer told herself that she could read hope in the faces of the Willises for the first time in a long while. It was because of Kinniston, of course. He gave them the steel they needed in their backbones.

When he saw her eyeing him, Kinniston said, "You too, Fay. You come along. You'll need food too, you know, for that ranch of yours."

She blinked. "My ranch?"

"That's a valuable property you have. You have steers roaming your grasslands. So they burned down your ranch house. I've known ranchers who worked out of tents for a spell, while they were building their ranch houses. Or lived in sod huts, for that matter."

Fay nodded slowly, her eyes held by the eyes of this man. Of course. She owned the land now, all the steers that grazed on the Triangle grassland. If what Kinniston said were to come true, if she could hold onto that property, she might be able to make a go of it.

She nodded. "I'll come."

While the men talked, the two women rose and gathered up the dishes, carrying them into the kitchen. Fay worked along with Clarissa Willis, and when they were done and she was hanging up the dish towel, she told herself that she wanted to find and talk with Abel Kinniston.

He was not in the parlor with the Willises, but outside, moving up and down, staring up at the stars. He turned as she came toward him.

"Did you mean what you said to those people?" she asked. "About helping them get what they needed in Wardance?"

"I meant it."

She moved closer, head up so she could look into his eyes. "But why? You're a lone wolf. You don't like people. All you can think about is vengeance."

Kinniston sighed and looked away across the land. "Came to me that I might hurt this Gib Young more by strengthening the little ranchers and the nesters." His smile was grave. "Worry him a little, before I kill him."

"Is that all?" she whispered.

His eyes came back to her. For a moment he hesitated, then he murmured, "Seems to me I've been riding lonely trails for too long a time. Might be a good idea to join the herd."

Her heart began to pound. "Meaning?"

Kinniston chuckled. "Been doing some thinking. A man can't cut himself off forever from his kind. Eventually he has to come back to the herd or be declared an outlaw. Never fancied the idea of being called an outlaw."

Her eyes fell before his. She had to take a deep breath before she could say, "Maybe you might even consider ranching?"

"Could be. And settling down to raise a family."

Her heart thudded wildly. She did not dare look at him for fear he would see what must be in her eyes.

In a small voice, she whispered, "A man needs a wife to raise a family."

"Thought of that, too."

Her gaze lifted for an instant to his, and then she felt the red flood rising into her face. She could not have spoken then for all the steers in Arizona. Or in Texas, for that matter. Fay drew a deep breath.

"You going to stay out here all night?" she breathed.

"Reckon it's best, in case Young sends any riders to attack this ranch as he did yours. I got my blanket, I'll sleep in it, off to one side, where that little knoll will shelter me from the wind."

"You'd be better off in a bed."

He shook his head, but he smiled. "Not yet. That will have to wait. Right now I'm like an ornery steer. Take some time for me to join the herd. You go on, now. You must be tired."

She nodded, reached out to touch his hand. Then she turned and walked back into the house, fighting for control of her emotions. Did he mean what she read into his words? Was he really thinking about settling down, getting married and raising some kids? Was he? Or was she just a foolish girl to read into his words something he had never intended?

At the door she turned. He was still standing there, looking after her. It struck Fay that he looked strangely lonely, standing there under the stars.

chapter eight

They came at sunup, in wagons trundling across the flats, riding horses or mules. Kinniston watched them as they moved toward the ranch house, studying them. Some were ranchers; these men rode horses or drove buckboards. The nesters and the settlers handled the reins for their wagons. Each man was armed with a rifle, and there were more than a few with handguns in holsters at their sides.

Jim Willis walked forward, inviting Kinniston to join him by a wave of his hand. The others drew up and watched as they approached.

"We're riding into Wardance after flour and butter, and whatever else we may be needing," he said.

Two riders from the Lazy K were looking at Kinniston. One of them asked, "He going with us?"

Willis nodded. "He's the ramrod."

Kinniston pushed forward. "Any shooting to be done, you leave it to me."

The men scowled, and one of them snapped, "I can hold up my end when it comes to swappin' bullets."

Kinniston smiled. "I've no doubt you can. But if I do any killing that's got to be done, I'm the man they'll come after."

"The hell with that. Let 'em come after all of us."

A chorus of growls told Kinniston that he might have a revolt on his hands if he insisted on crowding them out of any fighting that might erupt. A warmth spread through him as his eyes took in these men.

This was their fight. No man was going to crowd them out of it. He chuckled, then nodded.

"Fair enough. I'm not a man to deny anybody his right to stand up for himself. If there's any fighting, you can all join in. So let's get moving."

His Nez Perce horse was saddled. He swung up into the kak and toed the horse into a trot, aware that Jim Willis was riding side by side with him and that Pete Barlow, who owned the Lazy K, was on his left.

Like that, they rode to Wardance.

The town was almost empty at this hour of the morning. The men who had ridden in off the ranges for drinks at the saloons, the miners who had been in the Desert Rose, were all gone now. The girls who had danced with them were asleep in their beds on the second stories of the saloons.

Here and there a head was poked out of swinging doors as a swamper or a barkeep, up and moving about even at this time of day, stared with wide eyes. Kinniston ignored their looks as he guided his mount toward a big general store.

He swung down and stood a moment, looking up and down the long single street of the town. Where was Dutch Korman, if he was the town marshal? No one approached them, no one called out or shouted.

"Get inside," he said to Jim Willis.

He waited as they crowded into the big store, to make their orders. Dutch ought to be somewhere about, since this was his town. Unless he was wrong in his assumption that Luther Kesselring was Dutch Korman? No matter. He would know as soon as he laid eyes on him.

Voices from inside the general store touched his ears. They were quarrelsome voices, raised in argument. What was wrong? He turned and glanced at the open doors.

Sighing, he moved forward, up onto the sundried wooden sidewalk. Then he was stepping into the big store, his eyes going at once to the proprietor, who stood with folded arms behind his long counter. The man was scowling blackly.

Kinniston moved forward, asking, "What's the problem."

It was young Joe Willis who answered. "He won't serve us. Claims he don't have what we want."

Kinniston walked to the counter, looked at the man behind it. "Fill the orders," he said softly.

"Can't. Got nothing of what they want."

Kinniston drew his Colt, held it so that its barrel was aimed right at the store owner's heart. "You got a choice, mister. Either you serve them and stay alive, or I shoot you down like the yellow dog you are and we help ourselves."

George Trent stared into the cold eyes of this man whose gun was pointing at his chest. He tried to swallow, but his mouth was suddenly too dry. The gun never wavered, and the eyes that held his own were like those of a hungry wolf.

"Make your play."

George Trent sighed. This one meant what he said; it was there in his eyes. Hell! His life was more important to him than obeying an edict laid down by Luther Kesselring. His shoulders lifted in a shrug.

"Guest I can fill their orders," he grunted.

"Do that. Anybody who has a complaint, you send to me. The name is Abel Kinniston. You hear it?"

Trent nodded and began lifting down boxes from

his shelves. Kinniston watched him a moment, then moved away, stepping out onto the sidewak and into the dustry street. His eyes raked the street, up and down.

All he saw was a dog scratching fleas, and here and there, in a doorway or a window, a curious face thrust out. He moved away from the store to stand in the middle of the dusty street, for there he could see the ends of that street and make out anyone who might be riding into town.

Behind him, men were moving in and out of the store, carrying sacks and bags, dropping them into buckboards and wagons, returning emptyhanded for more. The few women who were with them were in the store, scanning their lists, checking to make certain that what was written down was the same as was being taken to the wagons.

The sun grew hotter on his shoulders.

The buckboards and the wagons were almost filled now. Only a few still remained. Yet always Kinniston stood in the middle of the street, waiting and watching.

He saw a dust cloud coming along the north trail and moved forward a few steps, watching. The dust cloud became three riders galloping abreast. These would probably be men from Gib Young's Fencepost, he told himself, since Fencepost was to the north.

As they neared the town, they slowed their headlong gallop and came walking. They eyes were taking in the wagons and the buckboards, and all the people thronging in front of the general store.

Their hands fell to their sixguns. They came on, their faces angry.

"Hey, you!" one man bellowed. "What in hell you think you're doing? Empty out those wagons—fast!"

"Keep loading," called Kinniston and began his walk toward the three horsemen.

Their eyes studied him, their faces growing darker

with fury. These men drew their pay from Fencepost, and they knew their boss. He had ordered that nobody was to sell the other ranchers and the nesters and farmers anything in Wardance. Those orders were being disregarded.

As one they swung down to stand facing Kinniston, and began moving toward him.

"You got a choice, mister," one of them snarled. "Either empty them wagons or go for your gun."

Kinniston smiled. "The wagons stay as they are."

They went for their guns.

Kinniston's hands seemed scarely to move, yet his big Colts were bucking and flame was running from their muzzles.

One of the three men went backward and fell. Another buckled and toppled forward. The third was spun around and dropped.

Young Joe Wilis swallowed hard. His eyes were wide; it seemed to him that his heart had stopped for an instant, just then. He looked at Kinniston and whispered softly, "I never saw him move."

A babble of words erupted, and men came crowding forward to stand with Kinniston.

Elwin Hammond, who owned the Bar 7, said softly, "This is going to mean war."

Kinniston said nothing, but he began to empty out the shells he had fired, and to refill the gun chambers with cartridges from his shellbelt. His eyes touched the faces of the men around him, studying them.

"Well?" he asked. "Ought I have let them bully you into emptying your wagons?"

Pete Barlow growled, "Of course not. If the Fencepost wants war, we'll stand ready. Our womenfolk ain't going to starve no more. You've taught us a lesson, mister. I'm grateful for it."

"Ought to have done this a long time ago," said another man.

Kinniston eyed them. "Fencepost may come to visit some of you, after this. I think we ought to band together. If they come we all face them."

"But how?" a man asked.

"Nobody knows where they'll hit first."

"They could wipe us out one by one."

Kinniston nodded. "Sure can, unless you do something about it."

Elwin Hammond looked hard at him. "You think you can protect us?"

"Sure can, if you do what I say."

Hammond looked around him at his fellow ranchers, at the farmers and the nesters. "I ain't takin' no vote, but I'll bet we're all agreed to follow your lead."

Heads began to nod. Kinnistow glanced into face after face, then gestured at the wagons. "Soon as they're all filled we move out of here in a body. Anybody tries to stop us gets killed."

He waited in the hot sunlight until the last wagon was loaded. Then his arm waved and they began moving out. When they were all on the way, he lifted into the saddle an nudged the Nez Perce to a walk.

When he was at the end of the street, he turned in the saddle and looked back. Men were emerging from the saloon now, moving toward the three still bodies on the street.

Word would reach Tom Yancey an Dutch Korman soon enough, now. They would know that war had been declared against them and their policies. It was up to them to make the next move.

The tiny town of Carbine dozed in the hot sunlight as Gib Young and Luther Kesselring swung down from their kaks and moved toward the saloon-hotel. They walked into the comparative darkness of the saloon and saw the barkeep straighten up and grin at them.

"What'll it be, gents?"

"Rotgut and information." Gib Young smiled.

A bottle slid toward them, with two glasses. It was Luther Kesselring who filled them, pushed a glass toward his friend. Then he said, "Heard tell that two friends of ours were shot down here a while back. You know anything about it?"

"Saw it all."

Gib Young stared at him. "He shoot them in the back?"

"No, sir. Face to face. They all went for their guns but—by the eternal!—that feller in them black clothes was like greased lightnin'. He shot them both fair and square. I never saw such shootin'."

Kesselring scowled. "Face to face, in an even match, he outshot French John and Bobby Cranford?"

The bartender shrugged. "Don't know their names, mister. But those two men who came in here looking for a girl were able to take care of themselves. Or so I figured when they came in."

Gib Young asked, "Did they know the man who bullied them?"

"One of 'em did. He whispered a name. Don't know if I made it out correctly. Sounded like Kinney or maybe Kinniston. Not sure."

Gib Young froze. *Kinniston*! Could it be that what this man said was true? Could Kinniston have come back from the grave? Could he be alive?

His eyes swung toward Luther Kesselring, who was staring at the bartender. Yes, Luther was hearing the same thing as he was. Kinniston was alive, and on their trail.

But why hadn't he come into Wardance?

Kesselring said, "Reckon we ought to go look at their graves, Gib." He lifted his glass and swallowed its contents in one gulp.

Then he turned on a heel and moved out of the batwing doors. Gib Young followed on his heels. They moved around the building and headed toward the two new graves they could make out under freshly turned sod.

Luther Kesselring said heavily, "There's no doubt of it now, Tom. It's Kinniston, all right. You know what that means."

Tom Yancey felt his heart beat wildly. He was not a fearful man, but any man who could gun down French John and Bobby Cranford in a face-to-face fight was almost inhuman.

And Kinniston was after him! After Dutch, too.

He stared into the face of his friend. "What are we going to do, Dutch?"

"Kill him all over again."

"Easy to say."

Luther Kesselring stared down at the two new graves. He was as worried as Tom Yancey, but there was nothing to do but face reality. If Abel Kinniston were alive and coming after them, they had to be ready for him.

"He's a loner," he muttered. "Always travels alone, never makes friends, never stays too much in one place. It ought to be easy enough to learn where he is."

"And when we do?" asked the other, bitterly.

"We shoot him down like we did before, from ambush."

Gib Young brightened. What Dutch had said was true enough. Kinniston was always by himself, he rode the back trails, he never had anything to do with people.

A man like that ought to be easy to get rid of.

The trouble was finding him.

He scowled blackly at the graves. Suppose Kinniston didn't wait to be found? Suppose he came riding into Fencepost land one night and walked into the ranch house? A cold shiver ran down his spine.

Even with his holdout gun, he didn't want to see Abel Kinniston go for his Colts.

"Dutch, we ought to stay together."

"How in hell can we? Sure, for a few days. But if I know Kinniston, he'll be like a wolf, out there in the darkness night after night, waiting his chance."

"Damn you. Don't be so cheerful."

"Only facing facts."

Gib Young nodded, feeling suddenly empty. All he had fought and strived for on this range was going to be taken away from him. His ranch, his cattle, his holdings in Wardance. They would mean nothing to him, once he was dead.

He drew a deep breath.

He had to stay alive. One way or another, he was not going to knuckle under to Abel Kinniston or any other man. Kinniston could be shot, he could die. It was up to him and Dutch to find a way to kill him.

"We got to make plans, Dutch."

Kesselring glanced at him, his lips twisted wryly. "How do you make plans against the wind, Tom? That's what he's like, the wind. He can come at us from any direciton."

"Then we got to be ready at all times." Gib Young sighed and moved away. "Come on, we'll go back to town and make our plans."

They mounted and rode off, side by side.

When they were still some distance from Wardance they saw the unusual activity in the street. Men were standing about, and some of the saloon women were there too, all talking. Gib Young straightned in the saddle.

"Never knew the town to be so active at this time of day," he commented.

"Never is. Wonder what's wrong?"

They cantered in and were met by George Trent. He walked toward them, his face still wearing a frightened look. The others came crowding after him.

"Mr. Young, it wasn't my fault."

Gib Young smiled. "I'm certain of it, George. But I don't savvy your drift. What do you mean?"

"Them ranchers come in today with wagons. They were joined by the nesters and the smaller ranchers. They come into my store and demanded that I fill their wagons with stuff they needed."

"You know my rules about that. Nothing to any of them."

"I know the rule and I was obeying it until that man came in."

"What man?" Luther Kesselring asked, leaning closer.

"Don't know his name, but he was wearing black and—"

Gib Young cursed. The profanity flew from his lips and the storekeeper stared at him, paling. He had been told never to serve any of those little ranchers and nesters. He had broken that rule and now he was going to be punished.

"He held a gun on me," he muttered.

Luther Kesselring smiled faintly. "He ain't mad at you, George, just at that man you was talking about. He's the one who gunned down French John and Bobby Cranford."

George Trent opened his mouth and held it open

even as his eyes grew big and round. He had seen both French John and Bobby Cranford go for their guns. He did not believe that any man—excepting always Sheriff Kesselring—was any faster.

"He backshot them, hey?" he gulped.

"No. It was a fair fight, him against the two of them. And he got them both."

"God! Who was he?"

"Man by the name of Abel Kinniston. Maybe the fastest gunhand there is."

There was something in the voice of Sheriff Kesselring that touched the store owner. His eyes went from his grim face to the angry, rather frightened face of Gib Young. What he read in that face quieted the turmoil inside him.

He stared a moment longer, then turned on a heel and walked away. Behind him, the sheriff glanced at his friend.

"We ain't dead yet, Tom," he whispered.

Gib Young roused himself from his musings. "Huh? Oh. No. But with Kinniston out there somewhere. . . ."

"He can die, like any other man. All we got to do is flush him out."

"You know what that means?"

"Sure I do. Men will die. What you and I got to do is try and arrange things so that you and me stay alive. We got to have a palaver, Tom."

He toed his horse to a walk and moved toward his house. After a moment, Gib Young went after him.

They dismounted in the yard and let the reins drop to the ground. Kesselring led the way, with Gib Young close on his heels. They walked into the house and the sheriff moved toward a sideboard, lifting a bottle and pouring two glasses half full of liquor. One glass he handed to his friend.

"Drink that. All of it. I know, I know. Bravery that comes out of a bottle ain't much good, but it's better than nothing. Now swallow it."

Gib Young regarded the liquor, shrugged, and raised the glass to his mouth. When he took the glass away it was empty. The raw liquor was like a fire inside him, building courage. He put the glass down and began to walk up and down the room.

"First thing we got to do is send the boys out after those little ranchers, farmers and nesters," Kesselring muttered.

Gib Young continued to walk. He was angry, yet afraid, and he was discovering that his wits—normally so quick and agile—were rusty. He glanced at his big blond friend and looked as though he had not heard him.

"Send the boys?" he repeated.

"We got to teach them a lesson. We got to get the upper hand. With Kinniston ramrodding them, they might get to feel that they can do just what they want around here. We got to break them."

Young nodded heavily. "Yes, you're right, of course. It's such a shock, learning Kinniston is still alive. . . ."

"Hell! He's only one man."

Gib Young's lips quirked into an ironic smile. "He ain't human, Dutch. By rights, he ought to be laying dead, back there on the Santa Fe trail."

"Well, he ain't."

The ranchman moved to a window and stared through it at the street of this town he owned. He knew enough of human nature to understand that if he and Dutch Korman died, the people in Wardance would soon transfer their allegiance to Abel Kinniston—if he stayed here—and those other ranchers.

And what would happen to his ranch?

Irritation merged with his fury. His shoulders moved as though throwing off a weight. He would not stand idle and let Kinniston come gunning for him. No! He would throw all his men against him and against those other men who had come riding into Wardance.

"We'll wipe them out, Dutch. The lot of them. And we'll get rid of Abel Kinniston at the same time."

Duth Korman smiled. This was better. This was the Tom Yancey he had always known, cold and unemotional, concerned only with his own welfare, with money that he hungered for, and ways of acquiring it.

"No reason why we can't. All it takes is a little planning, and you're the man to make those plans."

Gib Young smiled. Yes, he still had his brain to count on. That brain had made him wealthy. It had given him a big ranch—well, he had his clever hands that could cheat so nimbly at poker to thank for that—and that same brain would figure out a way to keep what he had won.

"I got to think, Dutch. I got to go back to the ranch and lay out a plan of attack. We're going to hit those ranches one after the other. We're going to kill the people in them. All of them. Men and women, same as we did with Shad Tremaine and with the Mercers. There will be no pity, none at all."

"Now you're talkin'."

Young chuckled. "Guess I was letting my imagination run away with me. I was spooked. But I'm not any more. We'll deal with Kinniston after we handle those ranchers and nesters."

He drew a deep breath. "Pretty soon we'll own the whole damn valley, Dutch. Then we can relax."

"After we get Kinniston."

"Yes, after we gun him down a second time."

"We'll stand over him and pump lead into him so

that there's no chance he's still alive."

Gib Young straightened, turned from the window and moved toward the door. He would get on his horse and ride back to Fencepost. He would call in all his men and send them out against the ranchers.

First the ranchers. After that the nesters and the farmers. He would make a wide sweep. He would burn houses, he would have his men shoot to kill. Nobody would escape him the way Fay Mercer had escaped.

With murder in his heart, he mounted up and rode away.

chapter nine

For two nights Joe Willis had sat the saddle of his fastest horse, here on the grazelands close to the Triangle ranchlands. Only at the first rays of dawn had he turned his horse and trotted away. Now he was here for the third night.

Kinniston was wrong. Gib Young was not going to make a move against them. He had accepted the fact that the ranchers and the nesters needed food; he had swallowed his pride.

Already there was grumbling among the men Kinniston had named to stay there on the Bar W. There was work needing to be done on their own holdings. It was useless to sit about and wait for Fencepost to come riding through the night to attack them.

Kinniston had made a mistake, that was—

Young Joe Willis stiffened. Was that a sound he had heard? He froze in the saddle, listening. Then he dismounted and put his ear to the ground.

Then he heard the drumming of hoofbeats.

Instantly he was up and into the kak, hammering his heels at his horse. Fencepost was coming, all right. In a little while its riders would be raiding his own home.

He rode his mount to exhaustion, but as he pulled into the ranch yard, Kinniston was there to meet him.

He slid from the saddle, gasping, "I heard 'em. They're on their way."

"Coming here?"

"Seems like. I didn't wait to ask 'em."

Kinniston smiled. "Good boy. Now get into the house. Rouse up everybody inside. They've been fretting and fuming at me because I've made them hole up here. Maybe now they'll change their minds."

He moved away toward where the Nez Perce horse was standing, head up and ears pricked forward. Joe Willis took a step after him.

"Where you goin?" he called.

"Going to make sure they're headed this way. You go on in the house and grab yourself a rifle."

Kinniston mounted and rode off in the direction from which Joe Willis had come. The way he figured it, Bar W would be the first ranch those men would hit. Bar W was the largest of the ranchers at whom Gib Young was hitting. There was Cling Magruder's spread, of course, over westward, and Carey's Double C. They lay in a line with the Bar W.

But Bar W had the most land. Hit the biggest of them first, then swallow up the others. Maybe fear would help against the others, once the Bar W was taken. That was the way Gib Young would reason.

Kinniston rode a couple of miles, then swung down and put his ear to the ground. Ah, they were heading this way, all right. Now he had to make certain it was the Bar W they were after.

He waited in the saddle, patient as any Indian.

In time he saw them, a long line of riders sweeping toward him. Kinniston smiled faintly. Nowhere else for them to go, riding as they were, except toward the Bar W. He had figured it out right.

He touched the Nez Perce horse and let it run.

He came into the yard, slapped the big horse into the barn, and then ran for the house, his Winchester in his hand.

As he stepped inside, Fay Mercer was there to meet him, her blue eyes wide. Her face was pale and Kinniston knew that she was frightened.

"Are they—is that the—"

He nodded. "They're on their way. Be here in a few minutes. You get into a back room and lie down, you hear?"

She eyed him. "And you?"

"I'll be with the others, fighting them. Oh, they're going to pay for this, and pay good."

She shivered at what she read in his eyes. He was more than ever like a kill-hungry wolf, lean and dangerous. Even the way he walked, as he moved past her into the front room where the men were gathered, guns in their hands.

She turned and fled.

Kinniston came into the front room and said softly, "They're coming. They aim to burn down the Bar W after killing the Willises, and after they do that, they intended to hit every one of your homes."

He paused, then asked in a flat voice, "You going to let them do that?"

A low growl was his answer.

He shifted the Winchester in his hands, then moved to a window. He peered out. In the darkness he could see little, but he knew that soon the front yard would be filled with shooting men.

The first attack would be against this room. None of those who rode to burn this house down knew what was waiting for them. As soon as riflefire met them, they would scatter.

"After their first attack, some of you boys get in

the other rooms," he said softly. "Somebody guard the rear door in case they make an attack there."

The silence deepened.

Into that silence a man murmured, "I been waitin' for a night like this for a long time."

Another echoed an agreement.

They heard the hoofbeats, the thunder of galloping. Rifles were lifted as men tensed at the windows. Somebody muttered, "Shoot to kill, damn their eyes!"

The yard was filled suddenly with men on horseback. As those men lifted their sixguns, the rifles began to speak. A thundering volley that rolled into a constant fusillade of shots made the room deafening.

Men dropped from their saddles, to lie still on the ground or crawl. One by one those saddles were emptied, either by rifle fire or by men who wanted the comparative security of the flat ground where they would not be seen so clearly. There was a lull in the shooting then. Somewhere outside a man was screaming in agony.

"Into the other rooms," Kinniston growled.

The men moved silently, crawling along the floor.

Kinniston watched the yard, his eyes boring here and there. He saw movement once, raised his rifle and fired. He heard a low groan and smiled ruthlessly.

They would make such attacks as these might unpopular around these parts. Once Fencepost learned that they were not going to be able to ride roughshod over these people, there might be a change in thinking.

Kinniston cared about that, but he was more concerned with Gib Young. Young was the brains and the will behind Fencepost. There would never be any peace while he lived.

"He won't live long," he told himself softly.

As soon as this attack was over, when he could assess the damages done to Fencepost, he would be able to make his own move against Tom Yancey and Dutch Korman. That would bring peace into this valley.

A bullet chipped splinters from the window frame where he was leaning. Kinniston marked the flash of light that showed where a rifle had been fired, and raised his Winchester.

A burst of firing from the rear of the house told him that an attack was being made there. He held his breath, listening. Yes, the defenders had apparently routed those running men. He sighted along his rifle barrel at the dark spot from which a bullet had come.

The dark blotch rose upward into the shape of a man. Kinniston put another bullet into the darkness, saw the shadow jerk and fall backward. His eyes went here and there, searching for other bits of extra darkness which showed where men might be lying.

He saw a man swing into the saddle, turn to flee. Someone to his right fired a Sharps buffalo gun, the roar booming loud in the room. The man in the saddle stiffend and pitched sideways, dropping to the ground.

"Teach 'em," somebody grunted.

Kinniston moved from the window, crossing the room at a crawl and sliding into the room where young Joe Willis was crouched down at a window, his rifle at the ready. He turned as Kinniston tapped his arm.

"See any of 'em?" he asked.

"Two. One's near the woodpile, the other's over there at the edge of the barn."

Kinniston slid to another window, peering out. He could make out a man lying flat behind the woodpile.

He murmured, "Keep your eye on the barn. Shoot anything that moves. I'll handle the one behind the woodpile. I got a notion they're going to fire the barn."

Joe Willis grunted and shifted his eyes.

Kinniston watched the man in back of the woodpile. The man was eyeing someone over near the barn, apparently waiting for a signal. Kinniston slid his rifle forward.

As the man slid forward and was bringing his rifle up, Kinniston slowly squeezed off his shot. The man rose upward, crying out. Kinniston shot once more and the man toppled sideways.

At the same time a dark blob began moving toward the barn door. Kinniston heard Joe Willis fire even as he triggered his own Winchester. The man took another step and lay flat. Kinniston put another bullet into him, to make sure.

"Good shooting, kid," he said to Joe Willis.

The youth flushed with pride. "I can hold up my end," he said.

"You sure can. You stay here and shoot at anything that moves out there. I'm going into another room."

He stood upright and moved forward. There was no one out there to shoot at him. Those two men were dead.

Fay Mercer stirred, where she crouched with the women.

"Abel?" she called softly.

"You rest easy, girl," he said. "Won't be too long now. We caught them by surprise. They're out there, those who are left, and they'll be mighty dangerous. Stay where you are for a while."

He moved into the kitchen, where three men were crouched down by the windows. They turned their heads to glance at him.

One of the men said, "There's four of 'em out there. Hidden by the well and the blacksmith shop."

Another man said, "We got them pinned down. They can't move or they die."

Kinniston smiled. "Good work. When the sun comes up we got them cold."

He went back into the big front room. Every man out there in the dark could not move without drawing rifle fire. They knew it; every man inside the house knew it.

Kinniston said, "We'll wait until morning. When the sun comes up they can't stay hidden very long."

Jim Willis grunted, then said, "I counted fifteen of 'em. Likely as not seven or eight of 'em are dead."

"Make that nine or ten. You boy and I got two out back."

Willis laughed softly. "Makes me kind of ashamed of myself, the way I've yelled at Joey for practicing so much with that gun of his."

"Man in these parts needs to know how to use a gun," Kinniston murmured. "You'd better say a few good words to him, come the morning."

"I will."

The night dragged on. The watchers in the house slept, after Kinniston passed the word. He went from man to man, tapping some on the shoulder, telling them to sleep now, while they could. He himself was not tired; he was used to staying up half the night or more, on his lonely rides.

Dawn came up over the mountains to the east, a great red ball of sun spreading illumination across the flatlands, over the ranch buildings. Kinniston watched it, his eyes sliding across the land to make out a huddled shape here and there.

As the sun brightened, those shapes began to move, seeking cover. Kinniston raised his Winchester and began pumping lead as fast as he could pull the trigger. A man went down, convulsing. Another lay where he was crawling, shot through the head. A third rose to his knees before falling sideways.

Firing rose out back. Kinniston abandoned his post to race toward the kitchen. Jim Willis was grinning and peering through the smoke toward the well.

"He won't make no more rides to shoot down innocent people," he said, then ducked as a bullet clipped the windowsill.

"Man out there can work a gun," somebody said.

Kinniston peered out. He saw the dead man to one side of the well and the blacksmith shop, where it leaned against the sunlight. A puff of smoke was being dissipated by the wind.

Kinniston said, "Those walls don't look any too strong. A man with a rifle ought to turn it into a sieve, if he started shooting at it."

Rufus Carey chuckled. "Been thinkin' much the same thing, myself. Shall we give it a try, boys?"

Three rifles sounded, sounded again.

They heard a man scream.

Kinniston worked his Winchester, keeping the windows clear. The men in there were not going to shoot back. These men beside him were fighting for their homes, their lives and the lives of their womenfolk, their sons and daughters. There was a grimness in his face as he kept working his trigger.

The three men with him kept shooting. Their bullets drove through the cheap boarding of the blacksmith shop and must have been working havoc in its small confines. Dust rose from the boards at the bullets went through them, and there was a desolate silence as Kinniston raised his arm and ordered a halt to the shooting.

"No sense wasting lead," he murmured.

The men rose from the cramped positions they had been holding and moved about the room to let their blood circulate better. Jim Willis looked at Kinniston.

"That ought to be the last of them. But how are we going to make sure?"

"That's my job," said Kinniston.

The others looked at him. It was Mike Pasternak who asked, "Why? It's just as important to the rest of us. We ought to choose to see who goes out there."

Abel Kinniston shook his head. "No offense meant, but this is a job for a man who's been a manhunter all his life, not for a rancher or a farmer."

He put his hands to his sixguns, lifted them slightly and dropped them back into their holsters. There was something so deadly, so assured, in his action that no one spoke. He lifted his rifle and moved toward the door into the big living room.

"You men got a job. You keep me covered. And—don't shoot me by mistake."

He walked through the living room and out the front door, aware that he was being watched by the men still in the house. Once he felt the sunlight on him, he dropped to the ground and began to crawl.

As he came around the side of the ranch house and saw the blacksmith shop, he paused for a moment, rifle pushed forward. There was no one at the window of the little shack, but there were gaping holes in its sides where rifle fire had cut away the dried boards.

A man in that shack could see him, if he peered through those jagged openings. Kinniston watched them carefully as he edged forward. He saw no sign of movement.

He was more than halfway to the blacksmith shack before he realized that the men in it must be shot up or maybe dead. Losing none of his caution, ready to leap and fire at the slightest hint of movement, he came to his feet.

Kinniston moved forward, rifle in his left hand, his right just brushing the butt of his Colt sixgun. Like that, he kept walking. He was tensed to draw and leap aside at the first sign of movement, and to fire at that movement, but nothing happened.

He came up to the shack, pushed against its lopsided door with his left hand. For a moment he stood there, crouched over, his gun in his right hand.

There were three bodies inside the shack, one off to the side, another that lay across the body of a third man. There was nothing to show any of them were alive. Yet Kinniston was cautious; he had known other men to fake death and then to move with blinding speed to shoot.

His eyes studied the three men. He saw where bullets had ripped into them, he saw the damage those bullets had done, and then he knew these men would never fire a gun again.

He straightened and waved an arm at the house. "Come and get them," he called.

The yard filled with men and women, all of them babbling as they stared. One by one the three men were carried out and placed side by side. Men brought other bodies, until Kinniston, standing quietly, counted fifteen.

"That's the lot," he said.

Rufus Carey said, "I'd never have believed it if I hadn't been here and seen it done." His eyes touched Kinniston almost with awe.

Mike Pasternak added, "We broke his back. We broke that Gib Young's back. These are all his hired gunhands. He's got nobody left."

It was Elwin Hammond who muttered dolefully, "He can get more. All he has to do is send for them."

Kinniston smiled. "That'll take time. He doesn't

have any time left." His eyes went around the men who crowded in close to him. "His days are ended. But I want to give him a present before I finish him off."

They stared at him.

Pete Barlow asked, "What sort of present?"

Kinniston gestured at the fifteen dead bodies. "These are the present. We'll tie them onto their horses and ride into Wardance with them. We'll leave them with that storekeeper for Gib Young when he comes to town."

The grim humor of it made the men smile.

"Is that wise?" Jim Willis asked. "It'll be like a declaration of war." He hesitated, grinned foolishly, then growled, "I guess war was declared quite some time ago."

"This is just a battle," Kinnistson said. "The last one, I hope."

Fay Mercer came pushing her way between the men, walking up to Kinniston. There was a subdued excitement about her.

"We're cooking breakfast, Abel. You'd best come and eat."

He hesitated a moment, then nodded. The men around him were watching him avidly. They knew his reputation, they understood that nothing had ever corraled Abel Kinniston, especially no female. And now Fay Mercer seemed trying to put her brand on him.

"Coming," he said softly, and when she turned, he went with her.

They ate in the big dining room, feasting on eggs and ham, on hot cakes smothered with syrup. They drank coffee by the gallon, and soon cigarette smoke was rising toward the ceiling.

Fay had seated Kinniston next to her, and it was her hands that served him. She knew well enough what the others were thinking. She was trying to rope him into marriage. Well, was she? she asked herself, flushing a little.

Of course she was. She felt she had been in love with him ever since that day at the creek, when Bobby Cranford had tried to keep her from reaching her clothes. The way Kinniston had scared off Bobby had done something to her.

Kinniston was like a rope-shy bronc. He would dodge and swerve and run, if given the chance. He had been a loner all his life. Was he ready now to accept double harness? Fay didn't know, but she told herself she meant to try.

She caught him looking at her as she leaned to take away his dishes, leaving him with a full cup of coffee. His lips twitched into a smile, as though in appreciation for what she had done. She smiled back at him.

Fay turned at the kitchen door to glance over her shoulder at him. His eyes were still on her. She turned and swung her hips at him as she moved into the kitchen.

Kinniston sighed.

Something was happening inside him. No longer did the lonely trails in the Big Horn and the Tetons, the Uintas and the Wasatch ranges, call to him as once they had done. He was growing tired of always riding on, across the great plains or skirting the edges of the deserts, a lonely man following lonesome trails on horseback.

Once he had met Dutch Korman and Tom Yancey, he would be done with his far travelings. Without the spur of vengeance to urge him on, what was left to him? A ranch, perhaps? A good woman, like that Fay Mercer? He signed again. Could be, could be.

He rose to his feet and moved out into the yard. The sun was hot already, touching his shirted shoulders. His eyes slid sideways toward that line of dead bodies.

Might as well tie them to the saddles they had come in when they were alive, and take them into town.

The other men were joining him now, lighting up pipes or cigarettes. Their eyes were on him, watchful. By unspoken consent, they had made him their ramrod. They were good men, most of them had families. They were here because they had defended property which was theirs, on which they had spent endless hours of toil and sweat.

For men like these, a man like him might seem a lobo, an untamed wolf. Yet he could change. He could become like one of them. Long ago he had tried to make such a change. Three men had stopped him.

One of those men was dead. Soon now, he hoped, he would meet the other two men. His hands went by instinct to his guns, and a hard look touched his bronzed face.

"Let's sling them on the saddles and get moving," he murmured.

They roped the bodies to the saddles, quieting the skittish horses, and then they swung up onto their own mounts. As they did, Fay Mercer came out into the sunlight, wiping her hands on a towel. Kinniston saw her, toed his Nez Perce horse closer.

"Be back soon," he told her. "Maybe we could have a talk then."

Her blue eyes were brilliant as they stared up into his. "I'll be waiting, Abel."

He swung his horse around and trotted away.

The others came behind him, the horses that carried the dead men trotting along. They rode with their rifles across their saddle pommels, but not one of them expected to have to use them. There was no threat against them in Wardance, and these dead bodies flopping on the saddles were proof enough that Gib Young had fired his best shot at them and missed.

Kinniston rode with his face always pointed ahead. There was an inner turmoil inside him, in which habit fought with intelligence. A man like him ought not to be thinking of a woman, especially a woman like Fay Mercer.

And yet—

The days of the long rider were at an end. Nobody wanted to hire a fast gun any more, or at least, not enough to make a difference. Be a good idea for him to hang up his guns, after he had confronted Tom Yancey and Dutch Korman. Maybe take up ranching.

Fay Mercer had a nice little spread. Might be added to, once Fencepost had no owner. He would claim to it, maybe. It would pay him back for the money Tom Yancey and those others had stolen from him.

They came into Wardance at high noon, and walked their horses down the street. Heads poked out of windows, around corners. Here and there a man came out of a saloon and stood watching them, eyes big and mouth open.

Kinniston brought his men to the general store.

He was swinging down from the kak when George Trent came out of his store. His eyes went to the dead bodies and he swallowed hard. Then he looked at Abel Kinniston.

Kinniston said, "Got a present for your boss."

"I got no boss."

Kinniston smiled thinly. "No? Then let's say I got a present for the man who owns Fencepost, whatever he calls himself."

George Trent felt numb inside. This man called Kinniston was like a package of dynamite that might go off if handled carelessly. He had no urge to set it off.

"Yes, sir. Whatever you say."

"You hand over these dead bodies to him. You tell him they're a gift from Abel Kinniston, a man he shot down from ambush and left for dead. You got that?"

Trent nodded. Suddenly he felt almost pity for the Fencepost owner. A man such as this one who stood before him was death on two legs. It emanated from him the way smoke did from wet wood when set on fire.

"I'll do that, sir," Trent found himself saying. "You can leave them right there, tied in the saddles. I'll send someone out to Fencepost."

Kinniston glanced around him. "You got a marshal in this town, a man by the name of Luther Kesselring?"

"We do."

"Where is he?"

"Out riding. I saw him leave about an hour ago. He's somewhere out there on the range."

Kinniston chuckled. "I can find him. Matter of act, I mean to do just that." His eyes touched the storekeeper. "When I do, this town will be needing a new marhsal."

George Trent nodded. It came to him that there was going to be a change in Wardance, and that when it happened this man before him was going to call the tune. Might not be a bad idea to let him know that if a change did come, George Trent was ready to change with it.

He cleared his throat. "Any of the men need anything?" he asked.

Kinniston grinned, but shook his head.

"Not today. Maybe tomorrow or next week. Especially next week."

"I'll be ready," the other said.

Kinniston swung around and moved toward his horse. Mounting up, he waved his arm, and the others fell in beside and behind him. Like that, they cantered out of Wardance.

chapter ten

Gib Young stood in his ranch yard and watched the little caravan of dead bodies on nervous horses come along the trail from Wardance. There was sheer disbelief in his eyes, in his rigid body.

He counted the bodies slowly. Fifteen. No, there was no mistake. Every man he had sent out against the Bar W was dead. Something was shriveling up inside him as he eyed those cadavers.

In one blow he had been stripped of all his gunhands, all the men who took his pay and who killed when he told them to. What was he going to do now? If only Dutch were here, with his calm judgment and cool words!

The man who rode before those horses, and who held a lariat that was attached to their bridles, drew rein before the Fencepost owner. He was a hanger-on at one of the saloons; sometimes he acted as a swamper, cleaning out the buildings. He was clad in dusty clothes, and his eyes were bleary, as though he had just gotten over a drunk.

He said to Gib Young, "George Trent paid me to bring these to you. He said to tell you a man named Abel Kinniston brought them in to Wardance."

"Kinniston," whispered Young.

"This Kinniston is out looking for Luther Kesselring right now, or will be. So he said, anyhow."

Young nodded. It was to be expected. What gnawed on his nerves was the fact that Kinneston had not as yet come gunning for him. But he would. Oh, yes, he would.

He waved a hand. "I'll get some of the boys to give me a hand with them. We'll bury them out back."

A sly look came into Buster Johnstone's face. "Got enough men left for that? Maybe I could give you a hand."

Young restrained his fury, aware that this man's insolence was but an indication of the way things were changing around Wardance. The people in that town were quick to sense moods. He, Gib Young, was in trouble. And the men who had fawned on him were ready to change sides.

It had always been like that. Why should he expect anything different now? Yet he told himself that if he killed Abel Kinniston, there would be sorry men in Wardance.

Aloud he said, "Sure. Why not? Earn yourself a ten spot."

He shouted for Little Crow, and between them they got the bodies off the saddles and began to dig the graves. As he worked with the others, Gib Young told himself that he was fair game, here on this ranch he had stolen and made his own.

All Kinniston would have to do was ride up to it and call him out, and then it was his gunhand against that of the other. In a fair fight, something told Gib Young, he would be no match for Abel Kinniston.

He had not practiced his draw every day, the way Dutch was accustomed to do. Even with that holdout gun, it was only an even break. He had never been a man to give another man an even break.

The sweat was standing out all over him by the time he had dug those graves, even with the Indian and Buster Johnstone to help. It was not just the work that made perspiration come out on him, it was his thoughts.

He knew he had not long to live.

When the bodies were in the graves, he left Johnstone and Little Crow to fill in the dirt. He himself walked back to the ranch house, entered it and stood a moment, scowling.

He would strap on the holdout and put another gun at his hip. He would get his Winchester and slip it into the boot on his saddle. Then he would ride away from Fencepost out onto the range.

Maybe he would see Kinniston at a distance and put a rifle bullet in him the way he had three years ago down there in Starvation Peak country. Damn fool that he was, why hadn't he walked closer so as to put another bullet between his eyes? That would have finished off Kinniston for sure.

Well, he would have his chance now. He would make sure of that. Out there under the sky, he would wait for Abel Kinniston and would drop him the way he would a mad dog. He felt better at that thought, and went out into the yard.

He shouted for Little Crow to saddle up his horse.

When the Indian brought the rangy gray, Gib Young said, "I'm riding off for a while. If anybody calls to see me, tell them that."

Crow nodded. His black eyes touched this man who paid him a salary, and he knew the man was afraid. Terror moved in him right along with his blood. Somehow, this pleased Crow. He stood and watched his boss ride out of the yard and head north, away from Wardance. He was running, the Indian knew. Running

155

away because he was scared.

Little Crow grinned.

Abel Kinniston walked with Fay Mercer across Bar W land toward a little creek. Their mounts stood ground-reined behind them at a short distance. Kinniston was uneasy. There was mild fright in him, and concern.

"Wanted to talk to you—alone," he muttered.

Fay Mercer nodded, smothering a smile. She knew well enough that Kinniston was uneasy because of her. The wrong word, even a faint grin, might send him away from her, never to return.

She moved toward the little creek, selecting a rock and seating herself on it. Her hand gestured at another rock nearby. She watched as Kinniston sank onto it.

"Been thinking," he said slowly. "Been telling myself a man like me has to settle down eventually."

Fay nodded, not looking at him.

"Only trouble is, I got to kill two men first," he added heavily.

"Why? Why must you?" she flared.

His smile was bitter. "If I don't, they'll come to kill me. I prefer to be the man that hunts and not the man that's being hunted."

Fay drew a deep breath. "You could go ranching with me. On Triangle. I can't do it by myself."

"Got me a better idea. We could combine your Triangle with my Fencepost."

Utter surprise made Fay gulp and stare at him. "*Your* Fencepost?"

"I've been thinking about it. When Gib Young is dead, Fencepost is up for grabs. I mean to be the man to grab it and hold onto it."

She could not speak, but could only eye him in

something like amazement. Fencepost! Why with her land and Fencepost, she and Kinniston would have the biggest spread in hundreds of miles. They would be rich. She sat there, bemused.

"Can you??" she asked at last.

"Who's to stop me? Gib Young will be dead, and I'll file claim to his land. Nobody around these parts will stop me. Nobody anywhere, for that matter."

She nodded slowly. "Yes, I guess it would be yours, then. You said once that you knew ranching. You could hire hands and make a go of it."

Kinniston glanced at her. "I'll be needing a partner." He waited, but she was staring down at her hands. He said again, "Been thinking about getting hitched to some woman."

She looked at him then. "*Some* woman?"

"You, then."

Fay Mercer was exasperated. Couldn't the man reach over and grab her, kiss her? Was he made of wood? She'd be damned if she'd throw herself at him, much as she wanted to.

"You think I'll marry you?" she asked.

Concern touched Abel Kinniston. He scowled. "You mean you won't? I thought—"

"Girl that gets married likes to know that her man will be with her, day after day and night after night, Would you?"

He nodded. "Just as soon as I find those two men, I sure will."

"I can't talk you out of going after them?"

He shook his head slowly. "A man owes a debt to himself, sometimes. I got me a debt to pay. Those men shot me and left me for dead. They also stole money from me. I figure that Fencepost will repay me for that money."

Fay Mercer came to her feet. She could not look at Kinniston; he would see the tears in her eyes. Had she found this man only to lose him to bullets from the guns of men like Gib Young and Luther Kesslering? In her heart, she prayed that he would say something, that he would go back on what he had just been telling her. She was tired of guns and killing.

She moved toward her horse.

Kinniston was there as she mounted up, standing to hold her stirrup. She looked down at him when she was in the saddle.

"I'll be staying at the Willises," she murmured, an reined the horse around.

As she rode away, she wept.

Kinnison watched her go, feeling vaguely lost. Never before had he had a woman who cared a fig whether he came or went, or even whether he lived or died, except perhaps his mother. His mother was long dead, and he had been accustomed to riding a lonely trail.

He swung up into the kak and nudged the appalousa to a trot. He did not follow Fay Mercer, however; he kept the 'palouse going in a different direction. He was not up to facing the girl again. He could not bear to look into her blue eyes and tell her he might be on his way to getting killed.

Kinniston rode as he had always ridden, easily in the kak and letting the Nez Perce horse run. Just so had he traveled from the Milk River country of Montana down into the Organ Peak land in the New Mexico Territory. Alone, with the sky overhead and the empty land around him.

He was tired of riding alone, tired of staring down into campfires and eating his meals with no one to talk to. He had not realized this until lately, when Fay

Mercer's face seemed always to be floating before his eyes.

He had never believed himself a marrying man. There had never been a woman who was willing to ride the trails with him, sharing his sort of life. Of course, he had never asked any woman to ride with him; he had never met any woman whom he wanted around him for any length of time.

Except for Fay Mercer.

He smiled wanly. Yes, he could visualize a life shared with her. He would not tire of seeing her face across a breakfast table or waiting in a ranch yard for him to come back from a long day's work with cattle.

He wondered if she would marry him.

Well, he would know that soon enough, after he had faced Dutch Korman and Tom Yancey. They had to die first before he would see the girl again. His hand went to his Winchester, drew it from its scabbard, examined it. Fully loaded, ready for use in case of need.

It would not be with rifles that he would gun down Dutch Korman or Tom Yancey. It would be with sixguns. Dutch Korman was a fast gun, maybe as fast as or even faster than he was himself. He would soon know the truth about that.

All day he rode, until he was in the foothills. He made camp then, as the shadows grew blacker and longer, and built a little fire to cook the rabbit he had shot.

He ate slowly, seated a little distance from the fire. If either Korman or Yancey were out there and saw his fire, they might come to investigate it. Let them come. He would be ready.

When he was done eating he built up the fire, but drew away from it a few yards until he was in almost total darkness. He lay down then and drew his blanket around him, keeping his Colt beside him.

He slept as he had always slept on the trail, with some part of him aware that the usual night sounds were around him. Like a wild animal, really. If there should be a cessation of those faint sounds, he would awake.

Dawn came to him with a rush of cool air moving the nearby manzanita bushes and the scrub oak. Kinniston sat up and, gripping his Colt, looked around him. He came to his feet then, shedding the blanket and moving toward the remains of his last night's fire.

He built another fire as his eyes ranged the land around him. Somewhere out there, Dutch Korman was waiting for him. In that town? Or out here where the chaparral grew?

Kinniston did not know, but he meant to learn.

Today he would ride into Wardance.

That was where he ought to find the town marshal. Kinniston smiled faintly at that. Dutch Korman was a thief, a gunman, a man without a conscience. As a marshal, he was ready to do whatever it might be that Tom Yancey told him to do.

Unless Yancey had given him other orders, he ought to be in town. It was there Kinniston would go. Now that the end of his long three-year search was near its end, he was in a hurry to bring it to a close.

Yet he made himself eat slowly, finishing off what he had left of the rabbit. He drank his coffee, rolling smokes to enjoy with it. Then he put out the fire, making certain no sparks were left.

He saddled the appalousa and rode on.

Wardance in midmorning was a quiet place. From a distance, as he reined up the palouse, Kinniston studied it. He saw a man or two walking, but neither of them walked the way Dutch Korman did.

He turned the Nez Perce horse and came toward

town from the side. Caution had always been foremost in Abel Kinniston; he saw no reason to abandon it now. He headed straight for the big store that George Trent owned.

Kinniston swung down from the kak and paused, waiting. His eyes touched the back of the store and he eyed the door set into its wall. Then he moved forward.

He opened the door and stepped into a room filled with boxes. He crossed the room and opened another door that gave entrance into the store proper.

George Trent turned, saw him. His eyes widened. He opened his mouth as though to speak and then closed it. There was no one else in the store.

Kinniston asked softly, "Is the marshal in town?"

"Yeah. He was in the Prairie Queen, last I saw him."

Kinniston nodded and moved toward the front window. He stood there, looking out. Behind him, George Trent did not trust himself to move. He stood frozen, scarcely breathing.

The street was empty now. No one moved. Kinniston fastened his stare on the front of the Prairie Queen, watching its swinging doors. If Dutch Korman were in there having drinks, he might be a long time.

Then the doors opened and the yellow-haired man came out onto the street. He stood a moment, staring up and down.

Kinniston moved out the door of the store and began his walk toward the man in front of the Prairie Queen.

Dutch Korman turned his head and saw him.

The big German froze. His eyes opened wider. This man who came walking so steadily, arms swinging at his sides, was a ghost out of the past. Until this moment, Dutch had not really believed that Kinniston was alive.

He had felt it was another man using his name and his black clothes.

But now there was no doubt.

This was the man he had left for dead, back there in the shadow of Starvation Peak. How could he be alive?

But he was alive, all right. And he was walking right toward him, his face cold and hard. For the first time in his life, Dutch Korman knew fear.

He turned slowly, aware that he might be going to die, right here and now. All he had to do was move his gunhand and he would find out.

He asked softly, "Is it really you?

"Don't waste time, Dutch. Make your play."

There was no hate, no pity, no emotion at all in the tones of this man in black. He was like a machine—a killing machine. No man had ever beaten his gunhand. No man who had faced this cold-faced killer had ever lived to tell of it.

Dutch moved his hand. The butt of his sixgun seemed to leap up and slap into his palm. The gun came out and started to lift.

A numbed corner of his brain told Dutch that he was too slow. My god! Kinniston was more than fast, he was greased lightning. His gun was up and spitting red flame at him.

Two bullets caught Dutch Korman in the middle of his chest. His gun fell from his suddenly nerveless fingers and he took a backward step.

He sat down in the dusty street and stared at Kinniston, who was holstering his gun and moving toward him, fumbling in the pocket of his vest.

He brought out an empty shellcase and held it so the sun glinted off it. Dutch Korman tried to talk and could not. He fell sideways and lay there.

Kinniston stepped forward, dropping the empty

shellcase on the body of this man he had hunted so long.

"Dutch Korman," he murmured softly, and let the empty cartridge drop. It hit Korman, rolled in the dust, and came to a stop against his dusty boot.

Kinniston raised his head and looked around. Heads were thrust from windows; a few men stood outside the saloons staring. Here and there, men whispered as they stared at Abel Kinniston.

He turned and moved around the side of the big grocery store to where he had left his horse. He was tensed, ready for the draw if anyone looked as if he meant to take up the cause of the dead mean.

But no one moved. The town was as still as death itself.

Kinniston swung up into the kak and toed the Nez Perce horse to a canter. Tom Yancey was out there, somewhere. He was going to find him and kill him, too.

chapter 11

Abel Kinniston came to Fencepost ranch in late afternoon, with sunlight making long shadows along the ground. His eyes had been examining the big ranch house as he neared it, but he saw no sign of life anywhere about. Yet Tom Yancy lived here; it was from this place that he had sent out his killers.

An Indian came into view as he neared the house. He stood and watched Kinniston approach, his head held high. Kinniston studied him gravely, lifted his hand and made the sign for peace.

Little Crow returned that sign, his black eyes going over this rider carefully. This was the man who was gunning for his boss, but there was no thought of fighting in the Piute.

"I'm looking for the man who runs this outfit," said Kinniston.

Little Crow shrugged. "He not here. He ride off with his guns and a good horse." Crow hesitated, then gestured northward. "He rode that way."

"When?"

"Yesterday, right after they brought in all the dead men."

Kinniston nodded. "Obliged."

He turned the Nez Perce horse and sent it at a canter along the little trail that went northward. There was no haste in Abel Kinniston; long ago he had learned the value of patience. He had been trailing this man for a long time; he was out there, somewhere in the distance. Sooner or later he would come up with him.

Until night fell across the land and the stars were high in the heavens, he rode. Then he found an outjut of rock surrounded by rocks, and here he swung down and made his camp.

There was grass for the horse, long bunch grass. He himself would finish what was left of the food he carried, make himself a pot of coffee. He stood a moment, his gaze ranging across the tumbled rocks, the grasslands that lay as far as a man could see.

There was no hiding place for a man out there on the grass. If Tom Yancey were anywhere around, he might be nested in these rocks. Kinniston lifted his Winchester from the boot and began to climb.

He went up high, until he could scan all the jumble of rocks. There was no one here but himself. He would unsaddle, let the appaloosa roam about eating, while he himself ate and drank. Then he would come back up here and sleep.

His night was uneventful.

He rose at dawn and scanned the countryside. Nothing moved there but his horse. Satisfied, he came down and made coffee, drinking it slowly. Today he would ride along the trail Tom Yancey had made, and he would come up with him. If not today, then tomorrow.

The anger that had driven him for the past three years had turned into a cold grimness. A man like Tom Yancey deserved to die; he was going to kill him. His hands flashed to his guns, lifted them out.

He smiled. His right arm was just as good now as it had ever been. His speed was there, the speed learned over the years by constant practice. That swiftness had kept him alive a score of times. Now it would get its final test.

Tom Yancey was no gunman. He was a gambler, or had been. And gamblers did not depend on a fast draw for safety, in case someone caught them cheating. He brooded over this fact as he sipped his coffee.

No, Tom Yancey would not go for a gun that hung on his hip. He would be more likely to have another gun hidden somewhere on his person. But it would be a gun that he could get into action fast.

Abel Kinniston thought hard. Then he sighed. "A hold-out," he murmured.

Yes. It would be like Yancey to have a gun up his sleeve. Yancey was a man who left little or nothing to chance; he would want all the advantage he could get. It would take all the speed of which Kinneston was capable to beat a hold-out gun.

He shrugged. No matter what sort of gun Tom Yancey carried, Kinniston was going to kill him, even if Yancey put a bullet in him. He had been shot before; he knew that usually it took more than one bullet to kill a man, unless it was placed exactly.

He saddled the palouse and mounted, then began his ride.

The sun was hot, the long grasses swished softly against his mount's fetlocks. His eyes touched those grasses, seeing where a hoof had stamped them down, where the going of the Fencepost horse had left its marks.

Yancey was not trying to hide his trail. It was there for anyone to see. Now why was that? Surely the Fencepost owner knew Kinniston would come after him. That was why he had fled.

To some spot of which he was aware, where a man

might lie hidden and gun down anyone? His eyes roamed the grasses, found no such place. Then it was further on, perhaps up there in the Ramparts. Kinniston tried to remember what he knew about those mountains.

He had gone over them a number of times. There was something about them that he should remember. As the Nez Perce horse cantered on, he bent his mind to the task of remembering.

There was a *tinaja*, a waterhole that might or might not have water in it. He recalled that much. And all around it were big rocks, seemingly pushed upward from the ground and tumbled about by a giant's hand. It was hot on those rocks, with the sun beating down on them pitilessly. He remembered seeing a wildcat lapping at water, last time he had been there.

That waterhole would make a good place for a man to stay beside, if he were being followed by someone with an urge to kill him. It would provide water, of course, assuming that there was water, and he might be able to shoot an animal or two and live on meat for a time.

The more he thought about it, the more convinced Abel Kinniston was that Tom Yancey had hidden himself there beside that *tinaja*. It was up high; it would give him a good view of the land around him.

He would be certain to see anyone who came hunting him.

Abruptly, he turned the appaloosa and sent him westward, to skirt the lower slopes of the hills, on a course that would bring him to one side of the *tinaja*. If Yancey were up there looking, he would see him, naturally.

Nothing he could do about that.

But he was out of rifle range, and he would continue his ride to keep himself far away from any rifle bullet. If Tom Yancey risked a shot, it would only prove to Kinniston that his deductions were right.

He took almost all the day to make his ride, but as the sun was sinking he was in the lower foothills of those Ramparts and moving steadily upward. He would not ride much further, he decided. He would swing down from the saddle and picket his horse, and then he would go on by foot.

Where some pine trees and Rocky Mountain juniper surrounded a level patch of grass, he halted. In a matter of minutes the saddle was off the palouse and it was picketed with a long rope.

"I'll be a while," he told it, in the fashion of the lonely rider who talked often to his horse.

He gave it a slap on its flank and then went upward, hidden from observation from above by the trees. He chose his way carefully, making certain that there were trees where he put his feet.

Kinniston smiled faintly. Tom Yancey ought to be worrying right about now, always figuring he was up there at that *tinaja*. He would have seen Kinniston riding toward him, gloating perhaps in the expectation that he would continue coming toward him so that Yancey could put lead into him.

He had seen him swing away, then, and move off in another direction. He would also know that he was down here, hidden by the trees, and that he was coming up.

"Sweat, damn you," he whispered.

He took his time. He was in no hurry. If Tom Yancey were up there, he would be there when Kinniston arrived. If he was not, then Kinniston would mount up and ride on.

He even paused, after a time, to light a cigarette and savor it. If Yancey could see the smoke, let him.

Kinniston was well hidden down here, with the tree foliage thick above him. Let Yancey wait and sweat.

He moved upward, between the trees and skirting the rocks. The air was colder up here, and after a time a wind sprang up.

Kinniston smiled. "Must be right chilly up there at that sink. There's no protection from the wind up there, the way there is here with all the trees."

He was more than halfway up when the stars came out. It was dark now, pitch black, with little or no moonlight. He could move freely if he wanted; Yancey wouldn't be able to see him.

After a time Kinniston paused and lay down on the ground. Might as well sleep. It pleased him to reflect that Tom Yancey would not dare to sleep, not knowing where Kinniston was or whether he might step out of a shadow suddenly and confront him.

He was smiling as he slept.

Kinniston woke to the chill of dawn, knowing the sharp bite of hunger. He was thirsty too, but he had his canteen with him, slung on its strap over a shoulder. He unscrewed the cap and took a long pull.

Afterward, knowing he had all the time in the world, he resumed his upward climb. He went warily now, making certain that his underfooting was soft and would not give off any sound. He wanted Tom Yancey to sweat, up there, he wanted him to be eyeing one direction and then another, and not be sure that Abel Kinniston would come at him from any one.

The sun rose higher in the sky. It was comfortable enough under the trees, but the sun would be baking that waterhole. Sweat would be running down Tom Yancey, all right. Let him bake a little more. No sense in rushing this.

Kinniston paused to light a cigarette, to smoke it to

a stub. He was not far from the *tinaja* now. He could be there in half an hour.

He stubbed out the butt and resumed his walking.

The closer he came to the *tinaja*, the slower he went. He paused often and just stood there, waiting, listening. He heard no sound. There was no longer any breeze. Everything was hushed, quiet.

And still Kinniston waited.

His back was to a tree bole, against which he leaned. His rifle was in a hand, ready to fire at a movement, a sound. The waterhole was nearby, just beyond those rocks. If Tom Yancey came to look for him, he would come out on either side of those big boulders.

Kinniston savored the moment. The last man of the three who had shot him down from ambush was before him—or so he thought. Two of those three men were dead by his bullets. Only one remained. Soon now he would pay the price.

He heard a pebble hit stone and roll.

Kinniston grinned. Tom Yancey was no outdoorsman, to make no sound when he moved. He was a town man, a gambler. He would have been better off holing up at his ranch or in one of the saloons in Wardance.

Make Kinniston come in to get him, where he was surrounded by men whom he could pay to backshoot an attacker. That was what he should have done. But maybe he was too excited to do any real thinking. A man with fear in his guts never can think very straight.

Kinniston straightened. "Yancey," he called.

There was a silence, then suddenly a scatter of stones. He had caught Tom Yancey by surprice. Yancey had stiffened, then had sprung for cover.

"I'm going to kill you, Yancey," he called.

There was no answer.

"Same way I killed Red Patsy and Dutch Korman."

"You're a liar!"

That sudden yell was harsh, and Kinniston caught the undernote of fear and worry in it. He waited a few minutes before shouting out, "Got Red Patsy at a little place this side of the Sawatches. That was how I learned where you were. He had a letter on him."

Tom Yancey did not speak, so Kinniston went on.

"Dropped Dutch day or two ago on the street in Wardance. Face to face, Yancey. He went for his guns and so did I. I was faster."

The sun beat down. Kinniston rolled a cigarette, lighted it, his eyes on the boulders. He struck a match, drew in smoke and let it out slowly. He had all the time in the world.

It was good to stand here and savor this moment, to know that whenever he chose to move he was going to face this man who had shot him down. They would stand face to face and it would be the speed of their gunhands that would determine who should live and who should die.

He drew in more smoke, let it drift out.

"You got a few more minutes left, Yancey," he called. "Then I'm coming for you."

"Come ahead, damn you. I can shoot a gun, too."

"Sure you can. But where are you hiding it, Yancey? Not in a holster—I'll make a bet on that. You got one hidden on you, haven't you? A hold-out, probably. Up your sleeve."

Tom Yancey shrank for an instant, his back to the warm stone boulder. How had Abel Kinniston known about his hold-out gun? Could Dutch Korman have talked? But no. Dutch would not speak about anything like that.

He drew a sleeve across his sweat-wet face. He had counted on surprise to let him gun down Kinniston. If Kinniston knew—or guessed—about his derringer, its effect would be lost.

He would never be able to beat Kinniston in a fair fight. He knew his own limitations, knew also the unbelievable speed with which Abel Kinniston could get a gun out and working. Whatever Kinniston shot at stayed shot, too.

He glanced around him. He was a damn fool to stay here, to remain and wait for Kinniston to make his move.

But he had nowhere to go. If he tried to make a break and run for it, Kinniston would hear him. But if he stayed here, he was going to be shot down inside a few minutes. The sweat ran down his face and his eyes glared at the sunbaked rocks around him.

He had fancied himself secure here. Up this high, he had a view of the land around. He had seen a rider yesterday, suspected it might be Kinniston. When the rider swung off the trail and moved westward, Yancey had cursed.

He ought to have left this place then and gone hunting him. But the fear in him had kept him glued here, telling himself that Kinniston would miss him and ride on, and that he might get in a shot at him when he came back.

Now it was too late.

Yancey listened, but he heard nothing. Kinniston might be moving toward him right now. His head went left and right, but he saw nothing except the rocks and the distant trees.

Tom Yancey pushed away from the hot boulders, backing up. He bent over and put the rifle down on the rocks. Kinniston would not shoot from ambush; he had a code. He would want to stand facing his enemy before he went for his Colts.

In an even break, he might still drop Kinniston. He was fast himself, with that hold-out gun. He could not believe any man could beat him. No, not even Kinniston.

"Come on," he shouted. "What the hell are you waiting for?"

He heard a chuckle. Then Kinniston called, "Giving you a few more minutes. I've waited three years for this. What's a few more minutes?"

Yancey cursed under his breath. Every minute that Kinniston waited was adding gall to his soul. He found that his hand was shaking and he tightened up his fingers, making a fist.

He backed away a little farther, until there was a good fifty feet between himself and those rocks. As soon as Kinniston showed, he was going to get that derringer out and begin shooting. He waited, tensing, then relaxing.

Where was the man?

As if he sensed his thoughts, Kinniston said, "I'm here, Yancey."

Tom Yancey swiveled his head. Kinniston was standing thirty feet away, under the branches of a big pine. How had he gotten there without Yancey's being able to see him?

Kinniston seemed almost to be lazing there, his hands by his sides, close to his gunbutts. Yancey blinked. It was Abel Kinniston, all right. They had been right, those people who said he had come back.

Tom Yancey shifted about to face him.

"It ends here, does it? All the years you've been searching for me? Doesn't seem right, somehow, that it should end like this."

He waited, tensing faintly. If he could catch that man in black off guard—"It ought to be out where people can see this, what I'm going to—"

Tom Yancey jerked his right arm. His derringer slid out into his palm and his finger was curling about the trigger. He was firing.

Kinniston seemed hardly to move but his guns were there in his hands and they were spitting lead at him. Those bullets hit into Tom Yancey and drove him back a step, then another.

Strange. He was firing down at the ground. His legs were weak. He was sinking slowly. His eyes saw the derringer in his hand and he tried to lift it. He had to kill someone. Who? Kinniston.

Yancey hit the ground and lay there. He heard footsteps. A moment later something hit him and fell to the rock beside him. An empty shell.

Tom Yancey died like that, with his eyes wide open.

Kinniston glanced down at his arm. A bullet had caught his sleeve and cut it as he had been twisting aside, firing and watching Yancey trigger his derringer. Good thing he had thought about that hold-out gun. Yancey was fast with it, damn fast.

Kinniston went hunting for his horse, brought it up and strapped Yancey's dead body on it. Then he led it down off the hills and went to get his appalousa. He would ride back to Fencepost with Yancey's body and see it was given burial.

Then he would search Fencepost. Could be that Tom Yancey kept cash on hand. If he did, Kinniston was going to take forty thousand dollars of it and ride off to Santa Fe to try to make a deal with the governor of the Territory.

After that—well, he would ride back to this range and maybe get himself married to Fay Mercer. He thought about that and his face lost a little of its grimness.

It was a long ride back to Fencepost, but he kept at it until he rode into the yard and saw men standing looking at him. Fay Mercer was with them. The men were all heavily armed.

Fay looked hard at him, then her eyes went to the body draped across the saddle on the horse trailing after him. Her eyes widened. Then she looked at Kinniston.

"You all right?" she asked.

He swung down from the kak and went to her. "I'm fine. Finished what I came here to do. Now I'm going into that ranch house and hunt me up some money—money that rightly belongs to me, since it was stolen from me."

Jim Willis was there with some of the other ranch owners. He cleared his throat, glancing around him at the faces of these men who had ridden with him.

He said, "Fay's been talking, Kinniston. Told us something about what Gib Young and Luther Kesselring did to you. We're backing you all the way."

Kinniston smiled. "Then come on inside." He explained that he wanted forty thousand dollars to take into Santa Fe. They nodded as they listened, and when Kinniston started for the house they went with him.

It took Kinniston only a few minutes to open the safe, the combination was in a drawer of the Philadelphia desk. In the safe he found a long narrow metal box. His eyes narrowed when he saw it, and he lifted it out with gentle fingers.

"This box is mine," he said softly, and pointed to where his initials were scratched into it., "I was carrying this box with forty thousand dollars inside it when I was gunned down and left for dead."

With a key from his pocket he opened the box.

The money was there, just as he had put it in, so long ago. He sighed and stared down at it, feeling Fay's hand on his shoulder. Slowly he counted it, then nodded.

"It's here, all of it," he said softly.

Fay said, "Then we can get married and go together into Santa Fe. I want to be there when the governor gets that money and tells you you don't have to worry about having been an outlaw."

He looked up at her, staring into her eyes.

There was happiness in those blue eyes. It was as if Fay were welcoming him home after a long trip. Warmth came into Abel Kinniston then and his hand sought hers and closed on it.

"Won't take long," he whispered. "Then we can get back here and set up housekeeping."

She nodded. "We'll make it into a honeymoon trip."

Kinniston smiled, closed the long green box and locked it. It was as if he were shutting away the past in his life. Now there was nothing to look forward to but the future, with this girl beside him as his wife.

We will send you a free catalog on request. Any titles not in your local book store can be purchased by mail. Send the price of the book plus 50¢ shipping charge to Belmont Tower Books, Two Park Avenue, New York, New York 10016.

Titles currently in print are available in quantity for industrial and sales promotion use at reduced rates. Address inquiries to our Promotion Department.